Sage Marlowe

The question "How far would you go to save the one you love?" is an excellent summary of what this book is about...If you like books about real men who struggle with real issues, if you don't mind reading about the raw emotions and issues that can result in, and how to deal with them, and if a love story where two men overcome a lot of obstacles is what you are looking for, you will probably like this short novel.
~ *Review From QMO Books*

*Total-E-Bound Publishing books by Sage Marlowe:*

Knives and Feathers

# SUB-MISSION

## SAGE MARLOWE

Sub-Mission
ISBN # 978-1-78184-517-2
©Copyright Sage Marlowe 2012
Cover Art by Lyn Taylor ©Copyright May 2012
Interior text design by Claire Siemaszkiewicz
Total-E-Bound Publishing

# SUB-MISSION

# Dedication

To F—both of you. You've truly changed my life.

# Chapter One

"He's a pretty thing, isn't he?" Robert observed, following Pierce's gaze, which kept lingering on the handsome man at the bar.

"Yeah, he's all right." Pierce shrugged.

"More like fucking hot, don't you think?" Robert enthused, and for once, Pierce agreed with him entirely. He let his gaze wander up those long, slender legs, the tight, leather-clad bottom and further up the hard line of the man's body to where his dark hair curled enticingly over the collar of his leather jacket. Although the stranger's back was currently turned towards him, Pierce had got a long enough glimpse of his face to know that it matched the attractive body. He was wondering if he should try to make a pass when the unwelcome feeling of being watched made him focus on Robert again. Apparently he was still waiting for an answer. "I already said he's all right, didn't I?"

"You fancy him." It wasn't a question.

"Well, I guess I wouldn't deny him, although the good-looking ones aren't necessarily good lays.

Besides, he might be covered in spots or have a hairy back." Pierce aimed to sound far more indifferent than he felt. He took another sip of his drink, knowing that he should slow down, but he was enjoying the sizzling, fizzy feeling it created in the pit of his stomach too much.

"I can assure you, what's underneath his clothes is just as pretty as his face. And he's a great lay."

"Is he?"

"Absolutely."

Pierce was about to dismiss it and just change the topic, but something in Robert's face as he eyed the beautiful stranger made him change his mind. He sighed and took the bait. "How would you know?"

Robert's expression turned smug. "I've had him. Repeatedly. He's all mine."

Pierce quickly raised his glass to hide the smirk on his face. Robert could be fun to talk to, and some of the guys at the club liked him as a Dom, but he also had a reputation for being a shameless show-off who'd make up stories to draw attention to himself.

"Yours?" Pierce didn't bother to keep the disbelief out of his voice this time. No way was someone who looked like the guy at the bar with someone like Robert. Especially not since everything about the man's body language, from the straight back and proudly raised head to the easy way he was talking to the bartender, stated that he was self-assured and strong—a confident, independent alpha male. Robert invariably wanted his men tame and submissive.

"Yes." Robert's tone and the expression on his face sent a shiver down Pierce's spine. "You don't believe me, do you?"

Pierce drew a hesitant breath. "Well, admittedly he doesn't look like your usual type," he answered warily.

"No? What does he look like, then?" There was definitely a nasty tone in Robert's voice but it wasn't angry, it was...challenging. Competitive. Pierce shrugged and thanked the waiter who had brought their refills. He didn't want to argue, but apparently Robert was determined to irritate him. And he was beginning to succeed.

"He just doesn't look like the submissive type to me."

"Looks can be deceptive," Robert replied idly.

"Yeah, well, you asked. If you ask me, that guy's a complete top. I don't think he'd so much as bottom for anyone, let alone submit. A pity really." Pierce took no small pride in the fact that he had an uncanny ability to not only instantly recognise whether a man was gay or not but to also figure out what they were like in bed within minutes. Before even trying to get them there. So far, he hadn't been wrong once. He drained half of his drink in one large gulp, preparing to end the conversation, when Robert gave him a malicious grin.

"Wanna do him?"

Pierce made an effort not to choke. "*What?*"

Robert's grin widened. "I'll let you fuck him if you want." Leaning in, he added, "And trust me, he *is* going to bottom."

Pierce's breath hitched as electricity jolted through his insides to explode in his groin. It had been ages since the mere thought of fucking someone had got him this turned on this quick. He'd had his fair share of experience and was used to being in control, and yet here he was, his trousers suddenly far too tight for comfort and he felt like a teenager hoping to get laid for the very first time. He stole a quick glance at the bar. Even though he knew he shouldn't be, he was interested. Very interested. The idea of exploring the slender, handsome body that lay underneath all that leather was enticing. He swallowed, grappling with his self-control, and stared at Robert. "Sure he's up to that? Shouldn't you maybe ask him if he's okay with it before you offer him to other people?"

Grinning triumphantly, Robert shrugged. "He's okay with whatever I tell him. I'll take that as a yes, then, shall I?"

His cock throbbing painfully in the confinement of his own leather trousers, Pierce took a deep breath. "Maybe you could introduce us first."

"My pleasure," Robert replied with an easy, slightly sharkish smirk and went to the bar.

Pierce's heartbeat sped up. He watched Robert walk up to the attractive stranger and slip a hand around his narrow waist. The guy stiffened but didn't move, apart from lowering his head so Robert could make himself heard over the background noise of the club. Whatever Robert told him made his head dart up and he took a step back. Following him easily, Robert invaded his space and pressed him against the solid wood of the bar. A small group of people passed Pierce, and he lost sight of the two men. When the others were gone, he saw Robert walking in his direction, the stranger following him like a docile puppy. *He's got him on a fucking leash*, Pierce realised with a jolt. The sight of a black, studded leather collar against the man's pale skin made his groin ache even more.

"Here we are, pet." Robert stopped in front of Pierce.

"Pierce, this is Noah. My new sub," he announced pompously and emphasised his point by giving the leash a little, sharp, unnecessary tug.

Noah flinched almost imperceptibly, but stood in perfect display posture. Back straight and shoulders squared, he held his head high and with pride. Only his eyes were downcast, trained firmly on the floor. All in all, he looked stunningly beautiful and as tame as over six feet of very well-proportioned man could look.

Pierce wondered how long he'd been in training. Although he himself had chosen to remain an outsider to the lifestyle, he knew enough about it to recognise and appreciate a well-trained sub. Noah certainly looked well trained so far, but, then again, looks *could* be deceptive.

"Hello, Noah," Pierce greeted softly. "Nice to meet you." He knew better than to expect an answer from Noah. It was Robert's call whether to order his sub to silence or allow him to speak. Surprisingly, Noah slipped up. He took a breath to answer and looked up, almost meeting Pierce's eyes before Robert reminded him of his position with another sharp tug on the leash. Noah winced, gasping audibly as the leather bit into the soft flesh of his neck. He instantly lowered his gaze back to the floor.

"I think that means you're going to remain silent for the rest of the evening now, pet, so you won't forget what you're supposed to do next time. Consider it training. You'll get your punishment for this later. After Pierce and I are done with you." Robert trailed a finger down Noah's cheek as he spoke, his voice a low and intimate whisper. The stern, almost malicious tinge in it sent another shiver down Pierce's spine.

He remembered that Robert had a reputation as an extremely strict and uncompromising Dom who believed that the liberal infliction of pain was the best teaching method. Noah seemed to have been taught a lot already. Once again, Pierce reminded himself that subs were in this because they wanted to be. Why grown men allowed themselves to be treated like that was still beyond him and he couldn't help wondering why Noah was in it. He didn't seem to be in need of someone who took care of his life for him so he was probably in it for the pain.

Noah had assumed his former perfect posture again and seemed entirely composed, but the heaving of his chest as he forced himself to breathe slowly and the flexing of the muscles in his jaw gave him away. *He's majorly pissed off.* Pierce wondered if Noah was angry about his own slip or Robert's disciplining of him. Maybe a bit of both. Most subs in training were very ambitious and hated making mistakes—although mostly not from fear of punishment but rather because they didn't want to disappoint their Master.

"So what do you think?" Robert glanced at Pierce invitingly. "Still wanna fuck him?"

Pierce swallowed nervously and looked at Noah, trying to read the expression on his face, which was nearly impossible without seeing the eyes. As far as he himself was concerned, the case was clear. Close up, Noah was even more handsome with his symmetrical features and the perfect angles of his face. The need to have him had become almost overwhelming. Still, Pierce would have liked a chance to ask Noah if he was really okay with it. Knowing he was not going to get that answer, he decided to rely on the basic fact of any Dom-sub relationship. It was the Dom who led the way, but the sub who decided how far they went.

If Noah really didn't want to do this, he could always use his safe word and end it.

"You know damn well I do," Pierce growled and ran his tongue across his bottom lip, anticipating the taste of Noah's luscious mouth.

Grinning appreciatively, Robert tightened his grip on Noah's leash. "Oh, there's one condition—I'll be watching. You okay with that?"

Pierce's stomach tightened. That was unexpected, although, if he was honest, he should have known there'd be a hook to the offer.

"I don't mind. Will he be okay with that?" He frowned, indicating Noah with his head. The thought of Robert watching him fuck Noah wasn't exactly a welcome one, but it could be worse—Robert wanting to get involved, for instance. It wasn't unusual that a Dom wanted to keep an eye on his sub if he let him play with someone else and it wouldn't be the first time that Pierce would've had an audience either.

"I told you, he's okay with anything I tell him to do." Robert's voice had assumed the authoritative tone Pierce had come to associate with a Dom in working mode. Pierce stole a glance at Noah, who still stood completely motionless. He hadn't failed to notice him shivering slightly at Robert's words. From anticipation or unease, Pierce couldn't tell. *He can stop this if it goes too far for him,* he reminded himself again.

"Fine. Rules?"

"Nothing that would put him out of service for more than a couple of hours. I know he's clean, but you'll use a condom and all the necessary precautions anyway. Apart from that, you can do anything you want with him. He's not allowed to speak as you've heard and I'm sure he's going to remember his basic rules better now. Won't you, pet?"

Noah gave a tiny, tight nod, eyes locked resolutely on the floor.

"Good boy." Robert grinned and slid a hand around the back of Noah's head, pulling him down to plant a domineering kiss on his mouth while giving the bulge in Noah's trousers a squeeze with his other hand. "Let's go. I can't wait to see you two together. It's gonna be so fucking hot." He turned, tugged on Noah's leash and led him to the stairs. If possible, the grin on his face had become even more disturbing in its smugness. He was well aware of being watched closely and enviously by most of the people nearby and Pierce finally understood. That was what this was all about. Robert was showing Noah off like a trophy, using his handsome toy to render himself more noteworthy and interesting. Noah should be well above letting himself be used like this, but apparently he was getting something out of it too. Pierce suppressed a sigh and watched Noah's buttocks move in front of him, still amazed that Robert had basically given him an all-clear with Noah. Not the wisest thing to do in the scene they were in. A lot of guys would gladly take him up on it, which might easily cause a scenario in which Noah's boundaries were pushed too far. Fortunately Pierce was far from doing anything extreme. All he wanted was to have some fun exploring Noah's beautiful body, then fuck him senseless. He didn't like hurting his lovers. Hopefully this wouldn't turn out to be a disappointment for Noah.

They reached the top floor, which contained the playrooms and the bedrooms. Pierce was relieved when Robert turned left, towards the aisle with the bedrooms. Tonight, he wanted it to be comfortable and preferred a decent, king-size bed to any of the fancy equipment the playrooms offered.

Robert unlocked the door to one of the rooms and led Noah inside. Pierce trailed behind, anticipation bubbling inside him as he thought about what he wanted to do to Noah.

"Here we are," Robert announced. He made Noah stand a few feet away from the huge bed in the middle of the room. A big, comfy chair stood in one corner, allowing a perfect view of the bed. Idly running Noah's leash through his fingers, Robert looked at Pierce expectantly.

"You know your way around, don't you? Toys and...stuff are in the top drawer."

"I know." Pierce focused on Noah, who stood in front of him in the middle of the room in his flawless posture, eyes locked on the floor.

"What are his safe words?"

"Huh?"

"What are his safe words?" Pierce repeated, mentally slapping himself for almost having forgotten the most important question when playing with a sub. He had to keep in mind that Noah was going to let him do anything, and he was trusting that Pierce would stop as soon as he said the word.

"Oh, um, butterfly." Robert choked out. Pierce shot him a look and grinned. Robert was already stroking himself through his trousers, his face flushed with excitement.

"Warning or stop?"

"Warning. He won't need the stop with you, because as soon as he's safe worded, that part's over."

"I'd prefer to know it anyway," Pierce insisted.

Robert sighed resignedly. "You are a control freak, aren't you? Pumpkin."

"I just stick to the protocol." Pierce smiled. "Okay. I'll just check with him." He turned to Noah. "Noah, are you clear on the rules? Your safe words are butterfly for a warning and pumpkin to stop altogether, right?"

Noah nodded.

"You'll use it as soon as you need me to stop whatever it is I'm doing and I'll back off instantly, I promise, okay?" Another weak nod.

"The sex between us will be over then. Do you agree with these rules?"

Noah let out his breath in a little gust and nodded his head.

"Okay. I suppose you're not allowed to meet my eyes but I want you to know that, as far as I'm concerned, I'm happy for you to look at me. You can even talk to me, but that's not my decision either." He was still trying to figure Noah out. Could that confident, proud exterior really be hiding a submissive personality? Well, there was just one way to find out. A pleasant way, hopefully.

"Clothes off, pet," Robert ordered softly. Noah obliged without hesitation, slipped out of the tight leather as smoothly as possible and stood up straight when he was done. The leather collar and leash were still on him, the sight and implication hugely erotic. Pierce had already decided to leave them on throughout.

"You've got him clamped?" he asked Robert, indicating the two vicious-looking pieces of metal attached to Noah's nipples. They were joined by a short, Y-shaped chain, the long end of which was attached to the collar. Pierce winced. This was a downright sadistic device. Every tug on the collar would cause the clamps to bite sharply into the sensitive flesh of Noah's nipples. And hurt like hell.

"Oh yes," Robert groaned.

"Maybe I should take them off." Pierce frowned.

"Leave them on."

"Are you sure? Looks pretty agonising."

"It is. But he likes it. Don't you, pet?" A tug on the chain had Noah hissing and twitching.

"Oh yeah," Robert purred into Noah's ear. "You're such a sweet little pain slut, aren't you?" He yanked the chain again and this time Noah couldn't suppress a pain-filled yelp. "Yeah, he likes it," Robert stated with a satisfied grin and turned to Pierce. "Your turn, big boy. I'm expecting a nice show." He winked and handed Noah's leash to Pierce. "Know what you'll do to him yet?" he asked impatiently. The prospect of watching Pierce with Noah seemed to be a huge turn on for him.

"Hm." Pierce fought his inner struggle silently for a moment. "To be honest, Robert, I'm not sure if I should do this," he admitted.

Robert gasped in surprise. "Why ever not? He's a fucking hot piece of arse and he's basically begging for it." His eyes glittered maliciously. "Would you like him to beg? I'd let him, you know."

Pierce shook his head and sighed. "No. I don't want him to beg. I'd love to fuck him, but I just can't give him what he wants. You know I'm just not into causing pain."

Robert shrugged. "Just warm him up a bit with a nice hard fuck and I'll take care of the rest when you're done with him."

Tuning Robert's presence out, Pierce ran his eyes down the length of Noah's torso and felt his reluctance vanish as his arousal kicked in with increased intensity. He clicked his tongue in approval as he started walking a slow circle around Noah. Robert hadn't promised too much. Noah's naked body certainly was a sight for sore eyes. Although his build was slender rather than bulky, his muscles were clearly defined underneath the smooth, pale skin. Pierce frowned as he spotted the thin, dark red welts that marred the flawless skin on Noah's back, from his shoulders down to his waist. They were in different stages of healing, some brand new, others almost faded. Probably at least one a day. There would be more, Pierce was sure.

He took a deep breath. More than anything else, the need to inflict pain or to have it inflicted was what kept him from joining the scene. He simply couldn't stand the thought of hurting a lover intentionally, no matter how much they wanted it. And those blows had definitely hurt. Pierce's guess was a bull-whip, reportedly one of Robert's favourite tools. Shuddering at the thought, he concentrated on mapping Noah's body with his eyes again. There was definitely no hair on Noah's back. There wasn't any on other decisive parts of his anatomy either. It just kept getting better. Pierce licked his lips. He hadn't failed to notice that Noah wasn't hard, but he intended to change that soon. A small step brought him right in front of Noah and he extended his hands, gently touching him for the first time. Noah quivered a little but stood perfectly still as Pierce ran his hands over his body. Yes, his skin was just as smooth to the touch as it looked.

Pierce trailed his fingers down Noah's chest to just below his belly button, then along his hips to that firm, well-shaped bottom and up again over his shoulders and to his neck. He curled the fingers of one hand around the back of Noah's head and pulled him closer. Noah resisted for a fragment of a second, then met Pierce's mouth. A groan escaped Pierce at that first contact. Noah's lips yielded under his and a wave of lust rushed through him. He pushed eagerly, opening Noah's reluctant mouth with his tongue and darted it inside. Warm, moist velvet welcomed him. Noah tasted very nice; of man with just a little minty something lingering on his breath. Moving his other hand to the small of Noah's back, Pierce pulled him closer and pressed their bodies together in a hard line. He rubbed his by now achingly hard cock against Noah's groin as he fucked Noah's sweet mouth with his tongue. When he felt lightheaded from lack of air, he pulled back and looked at Noah again. Flushed and a little breathless, Noah looked sexier than ever and his body was beginning to show some interest at last.

"On your knees." Pierce barely recognised his own gruff voice. Noah obeyed smoothly, still keeping his eyes on the floor.

"Open your mouth." Noah didn't need to be told what to do next.

Pierce groaned as Noah took him in surprisingly deeply and instantly built up a nice, firm suction combined with a slow but steady rhythm.

"Oh fuck," Pierce panted, thrusting his hips. No way was he going to last if Noah kept working him like this. "Easy, baby. I've got a bit more planned for you."

Either Noah didn't listen or chose not to obey, because he increased speed and suction a little, effectively drawing all coherent thoughts from Pierce's brain.

"Noah, oh fuck, yes, that's good... Stop it, baby, stop...it," Pierce stammered, wondering if Noah would do as he was told and if he really wanted him to. The sweet, wet heat of that mouth engulfing him felt just too good.

"Stop it!" Just before Pierce reached the point of no return, Noah stopped and let go. Pierce looked down at him, feeling dazed and shaky. He was yearning to see Noah looking up at him, but knew he wasn't going to get that so he cleared his voice to give the next order. "Get your sweet arse into bed so I can fuck it."

Noah got up in a fluent, cat-like movement and stalked to the bed. He didn't wait for further instructions, just settled on his hands and knees with slightly parted legs, offering himself to Pierce. The sight of him was so sexy that Pierce almost came right that minute. Clinging on to his self-control, he took the few steps to the bed. Then he opened the drawer and sorted through the variety of dildos, restraints, cock rings — and the more exotic toys he wouldn't ever dare trying out with a stranger — until he found the lube and condom he wanted.

"Anything you need from here, baby? Do you want a ring?" Pierce asked softly. The idea of putting a ring on Noah's reluctant cock held a certain appeal. Before Noah had a chance to answer, Robert's husky voice broke the stillness of the room. "Don't ask — just put a fucking ring on him. Why do you think I keep him shaved?"

"Shut up. You said you wanted to watch. Watching doesn't involve talking," Pierce grumbled and promptly decided against using a cock ring. He moved down the bed to kneel behind Noah, feasting on the sight in front of him. The man was just too beautiful. Pierce ran his hand over the perfect swell of Noah's buttocks, caressing him with the gentleness of his touch. It would get rough soon enough. He briefly contemplated stretching his own boundaries a bit to give Noah a little spanking, but decided against it. The rules were his and if Noah wanted that kind of treatment he'd have to wait for Robert to give it to him. He clipped the end of Noah's leash to the rail on the headrest, adjusting the length so that it wasn't stretched but short enough to allow Noah to pull against its hold. That way, it was up to Noah to decide how much he wanted to torture himself with the clamps.

Pierce squirted some lube on his fingers and went to prepare Noah. Excited as he was, he really didn't want to spend much time getting his lover ready but he didn't know how much Noah could handle and didn't want to take any chances. He gently pushed a tentative finger into Noah's body.

"Is he tight? Tell me, how does it feel?" Robert's hoarse, urgent voice interrupted.

"He's fucking tight. He'd probably rip off my cock if I fucked him now," Pierce snarled back, trying to get Noah's unwilling muscles to relax.

Robert moaned, his breath coming in time with the slow strokes on his own cock. "You lucky bastard, I know exactly what you mean. I haven't had him today yet. Amazing how he's still as tight as a virgin, like it's his first time, isn't it?"

Pierce huffed but didn't answer, refusing to let Robert invade any further. Yes, Noah was tight. Very tight. It would take a lot longer to get him ready than Pierce had anticipated, but he was determined to give Noah's body all the time it needed to open up for him, regardless of how much control it took.

By the time he had managed to get a second finger in, Robert's patience seemed to have expired. "Just fuck him, Pierce, will you?" he grumbled harshly.

"He's not ready and I don't want to hurt him," Pierce shot back, twisting his fingers this way and that, trying to overcome Noah's tenseness.

Robert chuckled sarcastically. "Remember he's a pain slut. He likes it fast and hard, don't you, Noah? Don't you want Pierce to give it to you just the way you like it?"

Noah jerked his shoulders in an indistinct motion.

"See?" Robert said smugly. "He wants you to take him now."

"For fuck's sake, Robert. Stop interfering or I'm out of this. I'm not gonna play rough with him if he doesn't tell me how far I can go himself, understood?"

Apparently Robert understood exactly how serious Pierce was. "Fine. Noah, tell him you're ready for a rough ride. Or would you rather I took over?"

Noah took a deep breath and swallowed. "Fuck me."

"You're gonna ache, you're not ready for my cock," Pierce warned.

"I can take it," Noah insisted quietly. Pierce wasn't entirely convinced, but decided to take Noah's word for it. The concept of pain was a difficult one. He unwrapped the condom and rolled it on, quickly slicking it up with a generous amount of lube. Angling himself, he slowly pushed in. He stilled for a moment, soaking up the heat while giving Noah's body some more time to accommodate him. The vice-like grip of Noah's muscles around his cock was almost unbearable and he knew there was no way he could hold back for long. He gave a first, probing thrust, watching the muscles in Noah's back ripple as Noah pushed back, allowing him in deeper. Soon Pierce let go and pounded into the tight, hot channel, grunting and groaning and far too aroused to hold back any more.

Noah remained eerily quiet. The only sounds from him were gasps and an occasional, half-suppressed grunt. Pierce would have preferred to watch Noah's face. Most of all he wanted to see his eyes when he came, but he wasn't going to complain as he slammed into Noah's body again and again. The firm grip of the satiny insides drove Pierce ever closer to the edge.

Sweating and breathless, Pierce knew he hadn't much time left. He wanted to watch Noah come even if he couldn't see his face. Changing his angle, he aimed for Noah's sweet spot and snaked an arm around Noah's waist, ready to make him fly. Noah gasped and bucked underneath him, twisting to shift his weight to one arm. The movement pulled at his leash and Noah screamed in pain, almost losing balance. He caught himself and shoved at Pierce's hand that had just found his cock and closed around it. It was barely semi-hard and Pierce felt a sting of disappointment.

Apparently Noah didn't appreciate his actions much. Again, he tried to find Noah's sweet spot, hoping that stimulating it would work its usual magic on him. Again, Noah shifted and shoved Pierce's hand away, blocking him with his own hand and arm. Pierce would have liked to know what that was about, but just then Noah flexed his muscles and pushed back again, squeezing him too tight and he lost control, shooting deep into Noah's body as he came with a harsh cry. Unable to hold himself up any longer, he collapsed on Noah who took his weight for a moment before gingerly lowering himself on the mattress as far as the leash allowed him to. Pierce felt utterly boneless and barely managed to pull out of Noah's warm body.

"That was...something," Pierce panted when speech returned. Noah was silent, crushed under him, but he was still breathing quickly and his heart hammered excitedly against Pierce's ribs. Pierce traced Noah's ribcage affectionately with one hand, loving how his skin felt sticky with their mingled sweat. Noah bucked up against him and Pierce took it as his signal to release him. Shifting to take his weight off Noah's slender body, he turned his head to look at Robert. He had completely forgotten about his presence for a while. Robert was still in the big chair, a wolfish grin on his broad red face.

"Short but very hot. Nice. Maybe next time you could try for a bit more show, though." He got up and walked over to the bed stiffly. "My turn. You can watch if you want."

"Huh? I thought you were long finished." Pierce stifled a yawn as he rolled out of bed, too tired to confront Robert about the constant intrusions.

Robert smirked. "See, that's the advantage of cock rings. They keep you hard for ages. Come on, Noah, get your pretty arse back up in the air." Before Noah had time to act, Robert ran his hand over Noah's bottom, then, without warning, smacked him firmly. The sound echoed in the silence that followed and a distinct red imprint welled up on the pale skin. "Nice, isn't it?" Robert whispered and repeated the action on Noah's other butt cheek. This time, Noah let out a low hiss. "Want me to fuck you now, pet?" Robert whispered. Pierce watched him, his insides tightening uncomfortably as Noah pushed up on his knees and gave a barely visible nod.

"Good boy. Now let's see if you manage to keep quiet this time. You already earned one stroke with the whip for screaming," Robert warned and traced the freshest welt on Noah's lower back with his finger. Noah flinched at the touch. Grinning, Robert rolled a condom on and shoved all the way into Noah's body in one swift motion, not bothering to add any more lube. Noah squirmed and gasped but remained silent even as Robert picked up the pace and thrust into him fiercely enough to bruise. Just as Pierce was wondering how much more Noah was willing to take, Robert pulled out of him, ripped the condom off and came with a wail, shooting his load all over Noah's back.

*He's marking him like a fucking animal.* Pierce felt faintly sick at the sight. He liked taking control in bed and he certainly had a possessive streak, but the way Robert domineered Noah made him highly uncomfortable. It wasn't the action itself as much as the expression on Robert's face as he watched Noah struggle to catch his breath. This wasn't a Dom giving his sub what they both needed. This was personal. Short, plump, balding Robert proving to himself that he could have one of the most attractive guys the club had ever seen and get away with fucking and humiliating him. In front of a witness. Pierce swore at his own stupidity. He should have known Robert had more in mind than just showing off his latest toy. The need to dominate seeped through Robert's pudgy little body like a disease. Worst of all, Pierce was beginning to have the unsettling feeling that this was not at all what Noah wanted. With one last, remorseful look at Noah's trembling, sweat and semen covered body, he fled from the room.

# Chapter Two

"Come on, lazy," Pierce scolded softly, dragging his reluctant dog along. "Only a little further and I'll let you go for a stroll."

He knew it was forbidden to let dogs run free in a public area, especially a park, but there was no one around who could mind and dear old June could really do with the exercise.

"Okay, now you can go, sweetheart." He unclipped June's leash and sent her off with a click of his tongue. June had clearly been waiting just for that moment. She sped down the path at an unusually fast pace, disappearing from Pierce's view. Just as he whistled for her to come back, he heard a high-pitched shriek, followed by fast footsteps and a much deeper, furious shout. *Fuck!* Pierce ran after the dog, hoping she hadn't caused any serious damage and cursing himself for not taking her further down the path to where he would've had a clear view. He sped around the bend and skidded to a halt, taking in the scene with a racing heart. A man was kneeling in the middle of the path, talking soothingly to the little girl standing in front of him. Tears streaked her pale cheeks and she snuffled, bravely trying to stop crying. June was bouncing excitedly around the man and the girl, trying to lick their faces.

Pierce stood frozen to the spot, hoping the little girl was crying only because she was startled, not because she was hurt. Unimpressed by Pierce's arrival, the man kept talking to her in a low, comforting voice. They were too far away for Pierce to make out what he was saying, but he found himself listening to the hushed voice anyway. It sounded nice. Soothing. Melodic, with a faint Irish accent. Pierce only realised that the man was talking to him when the soft drawl grew in volume.

"Uh, sorry?" Pierce asked, confused.

"I said how about you call your dog off now?" The man repeated. His voice was still low and soft, but there was an unmistakable edge in it.

"Yes, sure. Sorry. June, here!" Reluctantly, the dog returned to him, tail wagging madly as Pierce attached the leash to her collar. "Stay here now." Pierce took a few steps closer to the two. "Look, I'm sorry. Really. I thought I was alone here and it was okay to let the dog have some fun. I didn't..." He fell silent when at last the man turned to face him and he recognised him instantly. Noah. Beautiful, contradictory Noah, looking up at him with all that defiance and suspicion in his eyes. Pierce swallowed nervously. Maybe it was a good thing he hadn't seen those eyes before. Icy blue and piercing, they made him feel as if they were staring right into his heart.

"Great," Noah grumbled as he got to his feet. "Hasn't it occurred to you that there's a reason it's prohibited to let dogs off the leash in public areas?" he snapped.

"I said I'm sorry, didn't I? What happened anyway? Is she hurt?" Pierce started trembling as reaction kicked in.

Noah ran his hand over the girl's head affectionately. "Your dog knocked her over. Her bum's a bit dirty and she scraped her hand, but she's more upset than hurt. Shush, it's okay, love," he whispered softly, stroking the girl's cheek with his thumb.

"I'm really sorry." Pierce tried again. "Anything I can do?"

"Sure — keep your dog on the leash in future," Noah answered in a clipped voice.

"I will. Um, can I buy her an ice cream or something?"

Noah frowned, but the child at his side made the decision for him. "Yes, please. May I?" Her eyes gleamed again as she looked up pleadingly, fright forgotten at the prospect of the treat. Sighing, Noah admitted defeat. "Fine. Yes. You can have some ice cream."

"I think there's a place just down this way." Pierce pointed down the main path.

"Actually, it's that way." Rolling his eyes, Noah turned into the opposite direction.

"Oh. I don't get to buy much ice cream when I'm out here, you know."

Noah made a quiet sound between a snort and a chuckle, but didn't say anything.

They had walked silently for a few steps when the girl turned to Pierce. "What kind of dog is that?"

"She's a Labrador. Her name is June," Pierce explained. "What's your name?"

"Phoebe."

"Phoebe? That sounds nice."

She glanced at the dog again and let out an amused little giggle. "June? Like the month?"

"Yes, just like the month." Pierce smiled affectionately. She was charming.

"My birthday is in June."

"Really? That's a funny coincidence."

"Coin-cy-what?" She gave him a puzzled look.

"A coincidence," Pierce repeated.

"What is that?" A frown appeared on her little face.

"Um, that's..." Pierce glanced at Noah helplessly. A tiny smile pulled at the corners of his sensuous mouth. He didn't look like he had any intention of coming to Pierce's rescue.

"It's when things that somehow have a connection get together," Pierce offered. She stared at him blankly.

"Something that happens by chance," Noah explained.

She seemed to be content with his explanation, or maybe she just didn't care anymore. Instead, she indicated the dog. "Can I pet her?"

"Sure. She's friendly. She likes children." Phoebe extended a tiny hand and stroked June's broad head, timidly at first, but she gained trust soon and twisted her fingers in the black fur. Pierce stole a glance at Noah, who was watching the scene with outward calm. Only the muscles working in his jaw hinted at the tension inside him. He clearly wasn't comfortable with the situation, but was allowing it to happen, ready to intervene as soon as necessary.

"I like her. She's so fluffy," Phoebe announced, smiling widely.

Noah relaxed a little but kept his guard as they continued walking.

Within minutes, they reached the small shop that sold ice creams and various other sweets. A guilty conscience had Pierce buying the largest, most fanciful ice cream cone the shop offered for Phoebe. He would have liked to get something for Noah too, but he refused stubbornly.

"I'm going to end up eating her leftovers anyway," Noah explained as they followed her back outside. She was happily licking the creamy sweet, all worries forgotten.

"She's a gorgeous little thing."

"Yeah, she is," Noah agreed, blue eyes following her as she went to the playground and sat on a swing, rocking gently while she ate her ice cream. They remained at the fence that surrounded the playground, Noah resting his arms casually on the top bar.

"How old is she?"

"Six."

Pierce sighed. He'd hoped to get a chance to talk, but Noah was down to monosyllabic answers. "You looking after her?"

Noah glanced at him briefly and nodded.

Great. Now Noah didn't even answer with words anymore.

"Aren't you a bit too old for a babysitter?"

"Probably." Noah sounded weary.

Pierce stole a sideways glance at him. Noah was squeezing the pressure point on the bridge of his nose with his thumb and index finger. Pierce had wondered about it before, but now he was really curious about Noah's age. He didn't look much older than twenty, but his I'm-in-charge attitude gave him the air of someone older than that. As did the faint shadows under his eyes. Searching his mind for something harmless and yet conversational to say, Pierce was relieved when Phoebe returned and stood in front of Noah. She held the melting ice cream away from her, an accusing expression on her face.

"Enough?" Noah smiled, taking the offensive sweet from her when she nodded. He slid his tongue around the cone to keep it from dripping on him. The gesture was fairly erotic and Pierce had a sudden vivid flashback of what exactly that tongue had done to him on another occasion. He shivered and quickly pushed the picture to the back of his mind, deciding not to watch Noah finish the ice cream. Instead, he concentrated on little Phoebe who stood next to Noah, small hands clutching his leg. She was really very pretty, but she also looked rather fragile. Her skin had a pallid tone instead of the proverbial rosy cheeks. Pierce wondered what exactly Noah had to do with the child. What if he was really her babysitter? That would make the matter of his age far more significant. Pierce inhaled nervously and looked at Noah again. He was young, but he must be eighteen at least to play at the club.

Catching his eye, Noah grimaced. "What's up?"

"Nothing."

Noah raised one eyebrow sceptically.

"I was just wondering..." Pierce began awkwardly, knowing that he hadn't done much to get into Noah's good books.

"What about?" Bending down, Noah picked Phoebe up and set her on his hip. She slipped her skinny arms around his neck and clung to him, resting her head on his shoulder. "Tired?" Noah asked tenderly.

She nodded and stifled a yawn.

"I'll take you home in a minute, okay?" Noah's voice was back to the soft murmur he'd used before.

"Okay." Phoebe nodded, watching Pierce from underneath her long, silky lashes, and suddenly he knew.

Seeing Phoebe relax in Noah's arms, it couldn't be any clearer. They had the same intense, bright blue eyes and delicate features. Phoebe looked softer and more childish, her cheeks too round to be able to tell if she had inherited Noah's high cheekbones. Her dark curls were long enough to bounce merrily, whereas Noah's hair was cut too short to reveal much of its natural tendency to coil up. His eyes met Noah's again. Noah must have been far too young.

"You were going to say something?" Noah reminded him, resting his chin on the top of Phoebe's head in an affectionate, protective gesture.

"Oh, um, yes. Right." Pierce smiled evasively.

Noah shifted his weight to his other leg. "I really need to take her home now."

"I know. I was just wondering if maybe…you'd like to meet sometime. We could go out if you want." He swallowed nervously. What was it about Noah that had him feeling like a schoolboy with a crush?

The expression on Noah's face was guarded. "Go out?" He sounded surprised and less pleased than Pierce would have liked.

"Yes. Dinner. Or ice cream, if you want," Pierce added with a smile.

"Why would you wanna go out with me?"

*Do you own a mirror?* "I'd like to talk to you about…things," Pierce said cautiously.

"I don't think there's anything we need to talk about," Noah answered, equally cautiously.

"Maybe you don't, but I do. I've been wondering about some things."

Noah shifted his weight again, tightening his grip around the child in his arms. The earlier defiance had returned to his eyes. "What do you want from me? A repetition of what happened last time? That's not going to happen."

"No!" Pierce quickly checked his voice. "I just... I'm having a bit of a hard time understanding what that was all about, and I was hoping that maybe you could give me some answers."

A nervous twitch started in Noah's right cheek. "Look, what happened was just..." he interrupted himself as Phoebe sighed sleepily and stirred in his hold, picking up on his tension.

"Fine. We can talk. I'll meet you tomorrow at seven. Harry's Bar. You know where that is?"

Pierce nodded.

Noah turned around and went away without another word, leaving Pierce with a brand new set of questions.

# Chapter Three

Pierce wasn't at all sure if Noah was going to turn up and it annoyed him more than he was willing to admit. Quarter past seven. He swirled the dark red liquid in his glass for the hundredth time when he felt someone step into his personal space.

"Hello."

Pierce turned his head and his heart skipped a beat. Noah looked dazzling. As he leaned on the bar, his casual posture set off his long, muscular legs and slender body. He was wearing jeans and a dark grey turtleneck jumper that contrasted nicely with the blue ice of his eyes.

"You're here," Pierce choked out.

"Yes. Sorry I'm late." Noah smiled apologetically. "Phoebe's dinner took a bit longer than I expected."

"It's okay. What would you like?"

Noah glanced at the wine in Pierce's glass and shrugged. "The same as you, I guess." Pierce gave the bartender a signal and looked at Noah again. He liked what he saw. A lot.

"How was your day?" Pierce asked, cautiously feeling his way around. He was relieved when Noah smiled, albeit a little guardedly. "Busy. How was yours?"

"The same. I'm glad you're here, by the way."

Noah gave a non-committal nod and took the glass the bartender handed him.

"What do you want?" He looked at Pierce, penetrating him with his cool blue gaze.

"I told you. I'd just like to talk to you."

Noah sipped his wine. "What about?"

"Anything. You, preferably."

"Me?" Noah sounded amused.

"Yes, you."

"Might be a short conversation. There isn't much to tell about me."

"I don't think so."

"Hm." Noah watched the wine glitter in his glass. "How's Phoebe?"

"Asleep by now, hopefully," Noah answered dryly.

"She's gorgeous. You must be very proud of her," Pierce coaxed.

"She is and I am."

"I'm really sorry about frightening her yesterday."

"You already said so."

"I know. I'm just relieved she didn't get hurt."

Noah made the funny half snort, half chuckle again and looked at Pierce, holding his eyes levelly. "Leave my daughter out of this. There's no need to butter me up, Pierce. If you want a fuck, just say so and we'll take this someplace else."

Pierce stared at him in surprise for a few moments, trying to read the expression on Noah's face. "You're serious, aren't you?"

Sipping more wine, Noah nodded. "Yes." The tip of his tongue slid out to wipe a stray drop of wine from his bottom lip and, suddenly, the atmosphere changed. Pierce hadn't even really thought about having sex with Noah, thinking he didn't stand much of a chance anyway. Noah had a child and, for all Pierce knew, a wife. Plus there was the matter of Noah's connection to Robert. Being involved in the BDSM scene and leading a vanilla life seemed enough to keep a guy occupied. Pierce would have liked to get a look at Noah's neck to check if there was a collar on it, but that jumper concealed it effectively. He didn't know how far along Noah's training had been at the time when they'd met all those months ago and whether he was still in the scene at all, but he figured that Robert would happily take his chance to put his collar on Noah's neck as soon as he got it. He settled for watching Noah's luscious mouth. This time, he didn't block the thoughts it inspired. He wanted that fuck. Very much indeed.

"What about Phoebe's mum?"

Noah tensed. "What about her?"

"Well, honestly, I'm very much interested in taking you up on your offer, but not if you're involved with someone."

Noah snorted and raised his eyebrows in a mocking smirk. "How considerate of you. No need to worry, though, there's no lovely little wife sitting at home waiting for me and crying her pretty eyes out because I'm not home yet."

"So you're not married?"

"Gosh, Pierce." Noah groaned, shaking his head. "I'm really not here for family chit-chat. If you want to get laid, it'd better be now, 'cause I haven't got all night. If you don't, just tell me now. It's okay if you've changed your mind, no hard feelings."

"You didn't answer my question."

Noah sighed again. "Am I married? No, I'm not. I'm a happy, single dad, free to do as I please and fuck who I want and that's all the answer you're going to get." He looked at Pierce with a challenging stare.

"Let's take this someplace else then," Pierce growled huskily.

Noah drained his glass, a wicked grin on his face. Pierce quickly settled the bill and followed him outside.

"Where do you live?"

Smiling, Noah shook his head. "I'd rather we go to your place."

Of course he would.

"It's not far. We can walk if you don't mind."

"I don't." Noah's voice was rough.

They had just walked around the corner and entered a quiet back road when Noah suddenly turned and launched himself at Pierce, pushing him back against a solid stone wall. Winded and surprised, Pierce was still trying to catch his breath when Noah pressed his hard body against his and attacked his mouth in a fierce kiss. His tongue pushed between Pierce's lips, demanding to be let in rather than waiting for permission. Pierce was happy enough to let him, and, although it wasn't the way he usually liked to play, it felt quite nice to have Noah's slick, strong tongue inside his mouth.

Noah was a good kisser. Curious and playful, it seemed he was trying to explore every inch of Pierce's mouth in between tangling their tongues together. Minutes passed until they both had to stop to catch their breath.

Cupping Noah's cheek with one hand, Pierce rubbed his thumb over Noah's kiss-swollen bottom lip. "You fucking tease," he panted.

"Not yet." Noah smirked and curled his fingers around Pierce's hand. "Let's take this inside before we get arrested."

Holding on to Noah's slender hand, Pierce dragged him the short distance down the road to his house. He had the front door open in record time and pulled Noah inside, barely able to hold back anymore. As soon as the door was shut, he pressed Noah against it and himself against Noah, reversing their earlier roles. Lowering his head for a kiss, he rubbed his aching hard-on against Noah's groin, pleased to feel the matching firm ridge there. Noah gasped at the friction and Pierce took the chance to slip his tongue into Noah's mouth, eager to reacquaint himself with its sweet warmth. The taste of red wine still lingered on Noah's breath, but wasn't strong enough to cover his own delicious flavour. He didn't know how long they stayed there like this, tongues sliding against each other, hips rocking, but he knew he needed to have Noah. All of him. Soon.

"Come on, baby, I'll show you the interesting parts of the house." Pierce barely recognised his own husky voice. Smiling lasciviously, Noah followed him up the stairs and into the bedroom, where Pierce instantly started tugging at his clothes. "Time to get those off, don't you think?"

"Oh yeah," Noah breathed, his own voice just as rough as Pierce's. They didn't bother with decorum as they hurried out of their clothes, leaving the floor cluttered with discarded garments. Pierce took a moment to appreciate the sight of Noah's beautiful, naked body before him. No collar. Good. And no problem getting and keeping it up this time. Even better.

"Get on the bed," he ordered softly.

Noah's eyebrow shot up, but he moved to the bed and lay down, stretching in a cat-like movement. Pierce followed and settled next to him. Reaching out, he touched Noah's chest and let his hand wander along that adorable body to caress the defined stomach muscles. Noah was in astonishingly good shape. No wonder if he constantly carried around a six-year-old. Pierce smiled approvingly. If that was what it took...

Deciding not to fuss around any longer, he took Noah's cock in his mouth. The ragged moan it drew from Noah was enough to tell him the thought was very much appreciated and he was pleased to find that Noah tasted good everywhere. He worked with a nice firm suction until Noah's breath came in gasps and his hips flexed in shallow thrusts.

Sliding his hand across Noah's firm butt, Pierce gave him a squeeze and ran a curious finger between his cheeks. Noah tensed under his touch. "Don't get any ideas."

"Hm-mm?" Pierce hummed around the hardness filling his mouth and looked up to meet Noah's eyes. They were dark and glazed over with lust, but hard as steel.

"I'm topping."

Pierce let go. "What?"

"I top."

"No you don't."

"I do. Always."

"No you don't," Pierce insisted and pointedly raised his eyebrows.

Noah's jaw tensed, acknowledging the message. "Yes I do," he growled through clenched teeth.

"You didn't mind bottoming for me and Robert the last time."

"I mind now. And it's not negotiable." Noah's clipped tone made it clear that he indeed wasn't going to discuss this.

"Tough, 'cause I don't bottom," Pierce shot back, frustrated. What the hell was up with Noah? *It was so much easier when he wasn't allowed to speak*, Pierce thought spitefully. He'd been looking forward to burying himself in that handsome, supple body ever since Noah had offered that fuck and he had thought Noah wanted the same. Apparently he didn't.

"So what now?"

Noah pushed up on one elbow. "We can settle for either a blow or a hand job. Unless you want to call it a night altogether, that is."

"Should I expect any other surprises?" Pierce asked quietly.

"Don't know." Noah moved down the bed, his face stopping inches from Pierce's. "Maybe you should just wait and see what happens." His voice was low and intimate and his warm breath caressed Pierce's jaw as Noah leaned in to kiss him. This time, Noah's kiss was slow and sensual. A tingling sensation crawled up Pierce's spine as Noah slid his hand between his legs, gently nudging his thighs apart. For a second he wondered if Noah would try to push boundaries, but the strong fingers just toyed with his balls for a while before climbing higher and curling around his straining cock.

Pierce gasped. Yes, Noah knew exactly how to do this. His grip was just tight enough. He had used Pierce's own lubricant to get him slippery and he made that wonderful little twist at the end of every stroke.

Groaning, Pierce realised he wasn't going to last. "Noah..." he tried to warn.

"Yes, baby, I'm here," Noah answered in a rasp.

Pierce felt the mattress bounce and suddenly Noah was on top of him, holding himself up on one arm. This was not at all how it was supposed to be, Pierce thought, as Noah settled his long legs between Pierce's thighs and pressed their groins together. Still, it felt good and strangely intimate to be pressed down by the weight of Noah's body. It felt even better when Noah shifted and wrapped his hand around both their cocks, working them against each other. Noah looked down and Pierce stared helplessly into his eyes, rattled by the strange situation that this man had put him in. He was used to taking control and being in charge in bed. Not that Noah wasn't very capable, but...

Pierce felt the tell-tale tingle in his groin and abandoned his thoughts, giving himself over to sensation as his climax gripped him and the world disappeared for a moment. He was faintly aware of Noah shuddering and bucking over him and the hoarse groan as he came. A nice sound, Pierce thought. Enjoying the aftershocks of this unexpectedly sweet release, he took a moment before he opened his eyes and looked up at Noah's flushed face.

"You okay?" There was a tiny crease between Noah's eyebrows. Pierce wanted to lift a hand to stroke it away, but he still felt boneless. And happy. He nodded contentedly. "Very much so. You?"

Noah smothered a yawn. "Fine." He pushed up to sitting, his frown deepening as he looked down at the semen splattered across his chest and stomach. Pierce suppressed a grin. It seemed that, defying gravity, most of their combined load had ended up on Noah.

"Bathroom?" Noah asked curtly.

"Just down the hall, first door to the left."

Noah left the room, treating Pierce to an enticing view of his naked bottom. Pierce sighed with regret. Sure, this had been good, but he would have preferred to fuck Noah through the floor anyway. Listening to the sound of water running in the bathroom, he once again wondered what had just happened. This had been the strangest case of role reversal he'd had in ages. Wasn't he supposed to be the one in control, just as Noah was supposed to be the submissive type? He hadn't been very submissive just then. The only thing that could possibly make this scenario any weirder would be Pierce getting his hopes up for a post-coital cuddle and sleep-over.

Thinking about it, the idea held a certain appeal. It would be nice to wake up with Noah's warm body in his bed. Maybe they could have another go before breakfast. He quickly interrupted his train of thoughts. What was wrong with him? He didn't even usually take a guy home, let alone let them sleep over and it had been a while since he'd had a steady lover who'd shared his bed on a regular basis. And yet...

Noah returned, bare feet shuffling on the wooden floor.

"Got everything cleaned up?" Pierce asked, watching Noah sort through the clothes on the floor.

"Yeah."

"Quite a mess, huh?"

Smiling, Noah nodded. "That's the downside to a hand job, I guess. The stuff just goes everywhere."

"It really does, doesn't it?"

Noah made a non-committal sound and slipped into his jeans.

"What are you doing?" Pierce asked.

Noah pulled the jumper over his head and sat on the side of the bed. He trailed a finger along Pierce's cheek in a strangely affectionate gesture. "You know what I'm doing." Noah's tone was soft and soothing. The same as he had used to calm Phoebe in the park yesterday. Noah was right—Pierce knew what he was doing. It just didn't work that way. Or did it?

"I just thought..." Pierce protested feebly, realising that he sounded just like any of the lovers he had left to clean up the mess shortly after he'd had his fun with them. He had just never expected this to happen to himself.

Shaking his head softly, Noah bent down and brushed a chaste kiss on Pierce's mouth. "No, you didn't." He got up and put his boots on.

"I guess this means I'll see you around," Pierce said hollowly.

Noah took a deep breath. "I don't think you will. Take care."

Pierce listened to the sound of Noah's footsteps down the stairs and the thud of the front door falling shut. For the first time in his life, he felt utterly used— and completely smitten.

# Chapter Four

"Good evening." Pierce quickly hid his disappointment behind a bright smile when an elderly woman opened the door, glancing at him myopically through thick lenses.

"Good evening," she replied, smiling.

"Um, does Noah Conway live here?"

"Yes." She eyed him a little suspiciously.

"Is he in?"

"I'm afraid he's not available right now."

Pierce didn't fail to notice how she evaded giving a direct answer. She wasn't making it easy for him.

"I've got something that belongs to him and I'd like to return it, you see," he explained.

"I'll make sure he gets it."

"I'd rather give it to him in person, if you don't mind."

She measured him up thoughtfully. "And you are?"

"My name is Pierce Hollister. Look, it's his wallet. He...um, lost it. I found it and I want to give it back to him, that's all."

"May I see it please?" Her tone was still friendly, but firm. Pierce sighed but fished Noah's wallet out of his pocket and held it out obediently, waggling it a little. "See? It's his. I'm not going to rob you or anything—I'd just like to give this back and maybe have a word or two with him, that's all."

She smiled at him apologetically. "I'm sorry, Mr Hollister, but one can't be careful enough these days. Would you like to come in? You can wait for Noah if you want, he should be back any minute. I'm Judith Mitchell, by the way."

"Yes, thank you, Mrs Mitchell."

"That would be Miss," she informed him, holding the door open for him. He followed her inside where a nice, homely cooking smell greeted him and reminded him that he had skipped lunch. On cue, his stomach let out a desperate rumble. Politely ignoring it, the woman led him down a short, narrow hallway into a small, but tidy and impeccably clean kitchen where she gestured for him to sit.

"Would you like some tea?"

"Yes, please."

She put a cup in front of him and poured his tea. After briefly rummaging through a cupboard, she returned with a small plate full of chocolate biscuits.

"Noah's favourite." She grinned, resting her forearms on the back of the chair in front of her.

"Mine too." Pierce smiled back.

"Really? What a nice coincidence. So how do you know Noah? I'm not sure if I've ever heard him mention you."

"Um, well, I don't really know him all that well, to be honest. We only met twice, briefly."

If she had any suspicions about the nature of their meeting, she kept them well hidden.

"Yes, I know. He doesn't often get out to meet people." She sighed regretfully. "A pity, at his age. He really shouldn't have to worry so much."

"Worry? About what?" Pierce probed softly. Maybe that nice woman would give him some of the answers to the questions he had never got to ask Noah.

"About..." She interrupted herself, letting the sentence hang in the air when they heard the front door open.

"Hey, honey, we're home!" Noah's cheerful voice echoed in the hall, followed by Phoebe's bubbly laughter. "Wait, milady, you have to take your coat off." More girlish laughter followed Noah's fairly good impression of a humble servant.

Some rustling of clothes and Phoebe whizzed into the kitchen. "Auntie Judy!" She bounced excitedly into the woman's arms and hugged her as tightly as her little arms would allow.

"Something smells delicious in here," Noah observed on entering. "Which is good, 'cause I'm starving and..." He fell silent when he saw Pierce sitting at the table, and stopped dead. His expression went from relaxed to surprised to guarded in an instant and his eyes darted to Judith. "What..."

"I'm just here to return your wallet, Noah." Pierce held the small leather object out for Noah to take. "You, um, lost it at...err, yesterday."

Noah quickly swallowed the comment he was clearly about to make. Whatever it was, it probably wasn't fit for Phoebe's ears.

"Great. I've been searching for the stupid thing everywhere." Their fingers brushed briefly when Noah took his wallet.

"Sorry. I only just found it when I got home from work tonight or I would have made sure you got it earlier." Finding it had been quite a pleasant surprise if he was honest, as it gave him a chance to see Noah again, although he had felt a little uncomfortable going through Noah's personal documents to find out his last name and address. He'd also taken a glimpse at Noah's date of birth. At only twenty-five, Noah was quite a bit younger than Pierce would have liked him to be, but older than he'd feared.

Noah sighed tiredly. "Thanks anyway. I appreciate it."

"Hello. How is June?" Regardless of the tension between the adults, Phoebe had marched up to Pierce and stood in front of him.

"June? She's fine. Well, probably not totally fine, since she's still waiting for her evening walk, but she's got a garden, so she'll be okay." Pierce chattered away, relieved that at least one person in the room seemed to be glad about his presence.

"Does she have her own garden?"

"No, it's my garden. But she gets to play in it during the day."

"Can we have a dog too, Daddy?"

Noah smothered a sigh and shot Pierce a slightly accusing glance. "I'm afraid not, Pheebs."

"Why not?" She went to him and, hugging his leg, stuck out her bottom lip in a little-girl pout. Noah picked her up and pressed his forehead to hers. "Because, pumpkin," he explained patiently, "we don't have the space and nobody's at home during the day, so the poor thing would just end up getting bored. Besides, a dog needs to be walked at least twice a day, even if you have a garden, which we don't. Sorry, love, but it's not possible." He kissed the tip of her nose and put her back on the ground.

"Time for dinner, everybody," Judith announced brightly. "Mr Hollister, would you care to join us? You must be hungry and there's certainly enough." She was completely oblivious to the sideways glance Noah aimed at her.

"Thank you, but I think I'll…"

"No, please stay," Noah said, quietly but firmly. "In fact, I think we could do with your help. I'm sure Judith has prepared way too much food. As always." A tiny smile lit up his face.

"Just trying to get a bit of meat on you, my dear," Judith replied, swatting his butt in passing as she moved to lay the table. "You're way too skinny."

"I'm not!" Noah rolled his eyes and carried the small stack of plates after her. Obviously it wasn't the first time they had had this conversation.

Dinner passed quickly, with most of the time being taken up by Phoebe's lengthy description of her afternoon at playgroup. The rest of the conversation revolved around everyday trivialities and the news. Pierce was surprised to find that he was enjoying himself a lot. He never would have guessed that dinner at a small, crowded kitchen table, listening to a child talk about her day, could be fun, but it was. Maybe it had something to do with the way Noah's handsome face lit up while he watched his daughter. He doted on her, that much was clear.

"Anything I can do?" Pierce offered, when dinner was officially over.

Noah looked at the big clock on the wall. "Well, it's a bit late already, so I'd appreciate if you could help Judith with the dishes, if you don't mind. Then I can take Pheebs up to bed."

"Sure." Pierce gave him a warm smile. "Goodnight, Phoebe. Sweet dreams."

"Goodnight." Yawning widely, she let Noah drag her into the hallway and up the stairs.

"I don't think I've ever met a child that age who doesn't protest when it's time to turn in—not that I've met many children that age at all, but I've got a nephew who's just turned eight. He kicks a fuss about going to bed almost always." Pierce smiled.

"She gets tired fast," Judith explained, running water into the sink. "Besides, Noah's got a pretty good hold over her."

"Must be tough for him to raise a child on his own," Pierce said carefully.

"It is. Ever since Phoebe's been in nursery school, it's got easier. He's got a decent job with pretty regular times and the money's okay now, too."

"What does he do?"

"Something with computers. Don't ask me what that means exactly, I've never got the hang of those awful machines."

"That doesn't sound so bad."

"Oh, it's definitely much better than all the part-time jobs as a waiter and what-not he did when Phoebe was just a toddler. That was really tough for him. Sometimes he'd work two jobs and try to look after her most of the time himself. And all that while putting himself through university."

"He's been to university?" Pierce asked, surprised.

"You sound like you didn't expect that." She smiled.

"Um, I haven't really thought about it. I guess I just figured that as a single parent he didn't have much chance at a career."

"He's awfully bright, you know," she said, with no small amount of pride in her voice. "And he had really good prospects—about the best he could have hoped for. I'm sure he would have made it big if it hadn't been for..." she interrupted herself.

"For what?" Pierce persisted gently.

"I think, given the circumstances, he's doing exceptionally fine." She sounded protective.

"Yes, definitely," Pierce agreed, casting a look around the neat, comfortable kitchen. "It's amazing to watch him with Phoebe, really. He's so good with her. And patient. He loves her to bits, doesn't he?"

"He adores her. He'd do anything for her. Fortunately he doesn't tend to spoil her rotten." Judith smiled kind-heartedly.

"Poor guy. I hope she doesn't pester him about wanting a dog anymore. I felt pretty guilty to have put that thought into her head, but I think he handled it really well. She seems to have accepted it."

She grinned. "Don't worry. She's brought it up before and she would have come up with it again sooner or later anyway. Today will certainly not be the last time he'll have to talk her out of it."

"Talk whom out of what?" Noah asked curiously, entering the kitchen.

"Phoebe of wanting a dog," Pierce explained, putting the last dish back into its place.

"Oh no, that isn't over yet." Noah's smile was resigned.

"You don't seem upset about it."

Noah shrugged. "It's just the way it is. She wants something and doesn't really understand why she can't have it. Want some more?" He indicated Pierce's empty glass.

"Yes, thank you."

"Is she asleep?" Judith enquired.

Noah nodded. "Conked out as soon as her head was on the pillow."

"I thought so. Okay, sweetheart, I'm off now." Smiling, she heaved a large bag over her shoulder and hugged Noah.

"Thank you, Judith. You have a nice evening. Take care." He pecked her on the cheek.

"Goodnight. Enjoy the evening." Smirking, she shot Pierce a conspiratorial wink, leaving him puzzled.

"You too, thank you. Goodnight."

The flat was oddly silent after the door had closed behind her.

"Am I imagining things or was I supposed to catch some deeper meaning to what she said just now?"

Noah grinned and took a sip of his water. "Judith? You're lucky she didn't get a chance to grill you."

"She doesn't look like she'd do that."

"Oh she would, believe me. She's unbelievably curious, but luckily she also knows when to shut up."

"Does she know?"

"What?"

"That you're...you know?"

"That I'm gay? Sure."

"And she's okay with it?"

"Yep."

"Really?"

"Didn't expect that, did you?" Noah smiled.

"Not really, to be honest. I think in her generation that was much more of a taboo than it is now, so it's quite surprising that she's okay with it. How old is she?"

"Seventy-two come September. Besides, she's gay too, so maybe that helps her understand."

Pierce snorted into his wine in surprise, drawing a laugh from Noah. It was a lovely sound.

"Didn't expect that either, did you?" Noah smirked when Pierce had caught his breath.

"Not at all. Gosh, I suppose that makes me a very narrow-minded person, doesn't it?"

"You're forgiven."

"What's her connection to you? I thought she was your grandma, but I guess I was wrong about that."

Noah's eyes glittered amusedly. "No, she's not my grandma. She used to be my nanny."

"And now she's looking after Phoebe — taking care of the next generation, so to speak?"

"Yep. She's a great help. I don't think I could manage without her."

"Still, you seem to manage well. I don't think I could have a job and take care of a child."

Noah shrugged. "Well, admittedly it was a bit tough when I was younger, but it's been okay since Phoebe's been in nursery school. That allows me to work during the day, and with Judith taking over for a couple of hours when I need her to, I'm coping."

"Judith said you work with computers. What exactly does that mean?"

"I'm a computer consultant, which basically means that I get to sort out other people's cock-ups."

"Really? Are you any good?"

"Define good." Noah smirked, draining his glass.

"Well, you see, I'm currently having a little problem with my laptop." Pierce grinned sheepishly. "I hate to bring it up now. I'm sure this happens to you all the time, doesn't it?"

Noah's smile widened. "Yup, it does. Pretty much. What kind of problem do you have?"

"It seems to boot okay when I switch it on, but then it gives me an error code and doesn't do much at all."

"What error code?"

"I've no idea. I had the computer geek at work look into it and he said it was probably some kind of virus, but he didn't know what it was and hence couldn't do anything about it."

"You have any important files on it?"

"Yeah. Quite a lot, to be honest, and that guy said he couldn't recover them, either."

Noah smirked. "This is just a guess. They're only on that laptop and you haven't made any backups, right?"

Pierce felt the colour rise in his cheeks as he nodded and Noah grinned.

"It could be a lot of things. You can just bring it over tomorrow night if you want. I'll take a look at it," Noah offered.

"That would be very nice of you. Sure you don't mind?"

"It's okay. It'd be great if you could make it after eight, though. Phoebe will hopefully be in bed by then so she won't get all excited about us having a guest again."

"Okay. Thanks."

"Easy. You don't know if I can help you yet."

"Oh, I'm willing to take any chance I get."

"Are you?" Noah's eyes glittered teasingly.

"Well, I've got the feeling that with you I'm in the right hands."

Pierce was just wondering if Noah was really flirting with him when Noah raised his head and listened for something.

"I'll be back in a sec, I'll just check on Phoebe. Why don't you go through there and get comfortable?"

"Sure."

Pierce wandered into the next room, taking his time to look around. The living room wasn't much bigger than the kitchen, but was just as neat. Noah kept a very clean house.

He turned around when he heard Noah's footsteps.

"Is she okay?"

"Yeah. I just thought I'd heard her cough." Leaning casually on the doorframe, Noah rubbed his forehead tiredly.

"Are you okay?"

"Yeah."

"You look pretty bushed." *And so fucking sexy I can't wait to get my hands on you.*

"Na, I'm okay. I had a long day, that's all."

"Do you want me to leave?"

Noah smiled and took a step closer. "No. No, really. Stay for a bit," he insisted, when Pierce raised his eyebrows doubtfully.

The husky tone in his voice made Pierce's spine tingle excitedly. Although maybe that was because Noah had just slipped his hand behind Pierce's head and was giving him a hard, demanding kiss.

"I've been longing to do this all night," Noah whispered when he pulled back.

"I've been longing to do some things too," Pierce said, wrapping one arm around Noah's waist and the other around his neck.

"Such as?" Noah asked in a sexy, teasing purr.

"Take you to bed again." Pierce kissed him again, taking his time to explore Noah's mouth.

"Sounds good," Noah panted.

"Play with that gorgeous body of yours." Another kiss drew a moan from Noah.

"Fuck you senseless," Pierce continued.

Noah stiffened in his hold. "Not quite what I had in mind."

Pierce wasn't surprised. He'd expected Noah to be at least reluctant. "What did you have in mind then, baby?" he whispered into Noah's ear in his best seductive voice.

Noah shuddered. "You on your knees. Sucking me off."

That hadn't exactly been a part of Pierce's fantasy, but the thought was still very appealing. "I think that can be arranged."

"Then get down to it." The order was given so smoothly that Pierce didn't even recognise it as such until he was on his knees and had Noah's hard cock peeled out of his jeans and in his mouth. He chose not to mind being told what to do, knowing that he would make Noah stop giving orders and beg to be taken soon enough. Anticipation added to Pierce's enthusiasm, and within minutes he had Noah panting and gasping, lean hips moving to meet every movement of his head. Just where he wanted him. He'd let Noah get the edge off, knowing that it would make the scenario he wanted last much longer.

"Fuck, baby, this...ungh, yeah...your mouth feels so good," Noah stammered.

Pierce made a soft humming sound deep in his throat, letting the vibration wash over Noah.

A long, ragged moan escaped Noah's mouth. He looked down at Pierce with dark, dilated eyes. "Can I...I...need to...yes, oh, please..."

Pierce nodded in silent triumph, enjoying the rush of power that came with the realisation that he could indeed make Noah beg. He wasn't at all prepared for Noah's next move and almost choked when Noah suddenly pushed deeper into his mouth. Holding Pierce's head steady with his hands, Noah started fucking Pierce's mouth with fast, shallow thrusts. Not deep enough to choke him, it was still invasive, uncomfortable and yet unexpectedly erotic to be taken like this. There wasn't much Pierce could do other than let Noah take control away from him. Much to his surprise, he found he enjoyed it.

"Pierce...can't...oh yes," Noah hissed as he came, shuddering and jerking and almost knocking Pierce off balance. His grip on Pierce's head loosened and turned into a soft hold. They remained in their position until they had both caught their breath. At last Noah's fingers shifted under Pierce's chin to gently tilt his face up and he bent down to kiss him, caressing Pierce's abused mouth with a soft, moist tongue.

"Sorry, I didn't mean to..." He held out his hand to help Pierce to his feet. "You okay?"

Pierce nodded a little shakily. "Yeah. You took me a bit by surprise there, though."

"Sorry," Noah repeated with a guilty smile and pulled Pierce closer. "How about we go to bed and I'll make it up to you?"

"That—oh," Pierce moaned when Noah's tongue dipped into the sensitive hollow at his throat. "That sounds very tempting." He followed Noah into his small bedroom upstairs, curious to find out what Noah had in mind, but sensing that his own plans were highly unlikely to be a part of it. Soon, that didn't matter anymore. Noah took his time exploring and caressing, building up a burning need inside Pierce before he gave a delicious demonstration of his impressive talent at giving head.

Sometime after their breathing had returned to normal, Pierce asked tentatively, "Do you want me to leave?"

"What?" Noah blinked drowsily. "Why?"

"Well, I just thought...maybe you'd rather I leave," Pierce explained. *Maybe you're still only in this for a bit of fun*, a tiny voice in his head said.

"No. No, stay. You've had too much to drink, so you shouldn't be driving anyway. It's gonna be one hell of a morning, though."

"Why's that?"

"Pheebs. I've never brought a guy home before, so I guess we'll have to be prepared for a lot of questions."

"You think?"

"Probably. But no need to worry about that now. What time do you have to get up?"

"I'll just go to the office whenever I'm ready. I'm an early riser anyway."

"Sounds good," Noah murmured sleepily and turned over. "Just sleep now." Pierce listened to Noah's slow, regular breathing for some time before he, too, fell asleep.

# Chapter Five

Pierce had overslept, something that hadn't happened to him in years. Noah's side of the bed was deserted and cold—he must have got up early and very quietly. Pierce stretched and rolled out of bed. He felt good. A bit sticky perhaps, but good. Very good. Happy. Hopefully the morning after wouldn't change that. He went to the bathroom and cleaned up the worst bits before he shuffled down the stairs to find Noah.

The kitchen was warm but empty apart from the smells of coffee and a faint trace of Noah's cologne. Pierce's chest tightened when he saw the note on the kitchen table. He stared at the unfamiliar scribble with apprehension until the words became clear.

'Good morning, sleepy. Hope you don't end up being late for work, but you looked too cute for me to wake you. There's coffee (it might still be warm, else just make some fresh) and you'll find breakfast in the fridge if you want. Feel free to take your time—and a shower, you might need it... Have a lovely day, N.'

Pierce wasn't sure what to make of this, but the next line lightened his mood considerably.

'P. S. I'd still be happy to take a look at your laptop and that cock-up tonight.'

Pierce wasn't entirely sure what to make of this either, but decided to assume that the double entendre was intentional. He left Noah's flat after thirty minutes, caffeinated, showered and giddy with the prospect of coming back to see Noah in the evening.

When he returned several tormenting hours at work later, he still felt giddy, but also unusually worried. What if Noah had changed his mind during the day? Maybe he had decided it had all been a mistake. Maybe his note that morning had just been written in the spur of the moment and he hadn't meant it. Or worse, he had expected Pierce to read between the lines and understand that he was being let down gently. *Yeah, and maybe he's just as excited about seeing you as you are about seeing him,* Pierce reassured himself as he rang the doorbell. The door was yanked open within less than three seconds. That might be a good sign.

"Hi there." Noah sounded just a little breathless.

"Hey." Blue ice locked with Pierce's gaze and for a moment he felt as if he was going to drown in it before he managed to come back to his senses. "You look stunning."

Noah blushed prettily. "Thanks. Come in." He held the door open for Pierce, who took a moment to drag his eyes off Noah and enter. "Are you sure you don't mind this?"

"No, not at all."

"How's Phoebe?"

"Asleep at last." Noah sighed and rolled his eyes, then turned around.

Following Noah through the narrow hallway, Pierce enjoyed the view of that tight, well-shaped derrière a lot, and the desire to have Noah in that particular way made him ache. He had already spent a very pleasurable ten minutes in his office fantasising about Noah's handsome body and had decided to try to get Noah into bed again. Only this time they would play by Pierce's rules, which had Noah in quite a different position from the one he'd been in the night before.

Noah led him into a tiny room that was apparently his office. It contained a big desk, a chair and several bookcases. A second table was cluttered with bits and pieces of electronic equipment and the carcasses of a few computers that had been ripped open. Colourful cables and parts were scattered around them like the guts of slaughtered animals.

Catching his eye, Noah grinned. "Looks like a massacre, huh? Don't worry, they were dead long before I severed them like this. So, where's the patient?"

Pierce unzipped the case that contained his precious laptop and took the slim black computer out.

"Here. Please be kind."

"I'll try not to cause too much pain, but there are no guarantees. It might get ugly." Noah gave him a beautiful, lopsided grin that had Pierce's heart pumping more blood into his groin.

"Ready?"

Pierce nodded a little sceptically, but handed his laptop to Noah, who glanced briefly at the small label and raised an eyebrow.

"Anything wrong?" Pierce asked.

"What exactly do you need this for?" Noah opened the lid and switched it on. It started booting with a contented whirr.

"Oh, just some office work. Documents, mostly. Some spreadsheets, a few presentations, but that's about it. Why?" he enquired, when an amused smirk appeared on Noah's face.

"Did you buy it yourself?"

"No. It's my work computer, so the computer guy at my company picked it out. Why?" he repeated.

"Because" — Noah watched the small screen carefully — "this is one of the most expensive computers you can find."

"Isn't it good?"

Noah shrugged. "It is. It's just that you probably haven't ever used half of what it can do because it's just too much for the average user." He frowned, still staring at the screen. "Oh."

"What?"

"I guess the guy at your office is right. Looks like a virus."

"Anything you can do about it?"

"There's always something you can do. You said you needed the files on it, right?"

"Yes, definitely."

Noah took a deep breath. "I thought so. Well, that makes it a bit more complicated. By the way, would you like something to drink?"

"Yeah, I would," Pierce said. "Actually, I brought something with me. I wasn't quite sure what to get you, so I just brought a bottle of wine. And some chocolates," he added, a little self-consciously. Was it okay to buy a guy chocolates? "I hope you like chocolate."

"I love it. But you didn't need to bring anything," Noah answered, looking pleased anyway.

"Well, I wanted to. I figured that working on my big cock-up might be more fun with a little lubrication."

Noah's breath caught and Pierce was pleased to see his eyes darken when arousal kicked in.

"You're…probably very right about that." Noah's voice had dropped a little. *Gotcha*, Pierce thought with satisfaction.

"I'll…err, get the glasses."

"I can get them. I already know where they are. You can start on the computer if you don't mind," Pierce offered.

"Okay." Noah shifted his attention to the laptop and took a breath. "Okay, baby. Let's play."

Grinning, Pierce left to get the glasses and open the bottle of wine. He'd splashed out on it, knowing it was a very good one and hoping that Noah would appreciate it. It would taste delicious on Noah's tongue. And perhaps even more delicious on Noah's… He should really get a grip on himself.

"Here you are." He handed Noah a glass. "Cheers."

"Cheers." Noah clinked glasses with him absently, one hand resting on the keyboard. He set the glass aside without drinking.

"How's it going?" Pierce stared at the screen without the least clue of what was going on. Nothing of what it showed him looked familiar.

"We'll get there, I think."

"Really?"

"Yep." Noah smiled and pointed at the screen as it went blank briefly and letters started racing on it.

"Sure that's a good thing?" Pierce asked uncertainly.

Noah stared at him, shaking his head. "You really don't know jack about computers, do you?"

"I know how to use them when they work the way they're supposed to do." Pierce shrugged. "It never did that with me, though." He indicated the galloping white letters.

"I didn't think it had." Noah focused on the screen. "It's going to take a while. I'll try to save your files, then I'll run a couple of scans and updates."

"Mind if I take a look around?" Pierce pointed at a collection of framed pictures on one of the walls that had caught his eye.

"No, sure, go ahead," Noah answered absently. "I'll just start copying the hard disk."

The photographs were mostly snapshots of Phoebe at different stages of her childhood, some of them with Noah or Judith. The similarity between father and daughter was even more obvious in the pictures. Pierce's gaze rested on a small photograph showing Noah with Phoebe as a baby. She looked tiny and fragile — he looked shy and far too young to have her.

"Nice shots." Pierce indicated the photographs with his head.

"Thanks." Noah had left his chair and stood next to Pierce.

"Phoebe definitely takes after you. You're really photogenic."

A slight blush crept into Noah's cheeks, making him look vulnerable and cute. Why did Noah have to be so unsettlingly beautiful? Pierce felt heat well up inside him. Suddenly he was very much aware of just how close Noah was beside him. Close enough for Pierce to feel the heat of his body. Pierce swallowed and cleared his throat a little awkwardly.

"How old were you when she was born?" He knew the answer, of course, but at least the question served as an introduction to that tricky topic.

"Nineteen." Noah shifted uncomfortably.

Pierce flinched. "That's really awfully young to have a child."

"It wasn't exactly family planning," Noah said in a tight voice, twisting around to hit a few of the laptop's keys.

"I'm not judging you, Noah." Pierce said softly. "I only think it must have been pretty tough for you to have a child when you were still just a teenager yourself."

"It hasn't always been easy but I wouldn't not have her for the world."

"I know. What about her mother?"

"Don't know and I don't care," Noah snapped.

"I suppose she doesn't keep in contact with the two of you?"

Noah let out an irritated snort. "She didn't want Pheebs—never even saw her. She carried her for nine months and gave birth to her and that was all the contact they ever had."

Pierce felt stunned. "What? Why?"

"She was too young, I guess. And the situation was…complicated, to say the least." Noah's voice was hollow and strangely detached.

"Because you two were so young?" Pierce probed.

"Among other things, yes."

"I don't mean to patronise, but Phoebe is very lucky to have you as a father, do you realise that?"

"What makes you say that?"

"It's just…you love her so much. It's impressive to witness."

Noah nodded slowly. "She's the love of my life."

"I know. And I'm sure she knows it too."

"I'd do anything for her, but…" he interrupted himself.

"But what?"

"But maybe that's not enough," Noah choked out. The sudden pain in his face made Pierce's chest tighten with emotion. He sensed that there was something Noah wasn't saying, but decided not to pursue it. Noah was upset enough already.

"Shh, Noah. Don't be so hard on yourself." Before he'd allowed himself to think about it, Pierce covered the small space between them and wrapped Noah up in a soft, comforting embrace. It took a few seconds, but at last he felt Noah lean into him and some of the tension leave his body. "It's okay, baby," he whispered soothingly into Noah's dark curls. "Everything's all right."

He wasn't sure if Noah was crying until Noah raised his head and looked at him, eyes troubled and reddened but dry. His bottom lip quivered slightly. Noah looked so lost and confused and for a fragment of a second Pierce hated himself, but he just couldn't resist. Cupping Noah's cheek with one hand, Pierce stroked that plump bottom lip with his thumb before he leaned in and put a soft kiss on Noah's mouth. He didn't know what reaction to expect from Noah, but he surely didn't expect him to respond the way he did. Noah kissed him back with fierce hunger and pressed firmly against Pierce, the movement of his hips unmistakable.

"Whoa, easy baby," Pierce breathed into the kiss, trying not to stagger under the weight of Noah's slender body as it pushed against his. It seemed that Noah was aroused beyond caring. He slid his hands down and started tugging impatiently at Pierce's belt.

Freeing himself of Noah's mouth, Pierce tried to catch his breath. "Noah," he warned. Not that he wouldn't happily take Noah right there on the floor, but the thought of Phoebe walking in on them did put him off a bit. "Bedroom?"

"Yeah." Noah's husky groan went straight to Pierce's already enthusiastic groin. Somehow they managed to stumble into Noah's bedroom without making too much noise. Noah carefully locked the door before he started another attack at Pierce, seemingly determined to get their clothes off. Within seconds, they were both naked and crashed on Noah's bed. Somehow Noah managed to end up on top of Pierce and he seemed to be everywhere, kissing and touching every inch of Pierce's body that he could get hold of. Pierce groaned. He did wonder why he let Noah get away with taking control again, but decided it felt too good to fight him for it just yet. He'd just humour him a little longer and then... He jerked as he felt Noah's hand between his legs—in a place it was most definitely not supposed to be. "Noah? What are you doing?"

Noah's answer came in a husky growl. "Please, baby. I wanna fuck you so much, it's killing me." The pressure of that naughty finger increased.

Pierce licked his suddenly very dry lips nervously. "Noah, I don't really...oh, fuck, yes!"

Noah's slick finger was inside him, teasing him and reminding him just how exciting it could feel to be touched there by a lover who knew what he was doing. And Noah knew. Stroking and twisting, he massaged the tight ring of muscles into relaxation.

"I'll make this good for you," Noah promised.

He pushed in a bit deeper and Pierce felt his body open up with astonishing ease. *Traitor*. Noah added a finger, still moving slowly but persistently, stretching Pierce further. He alternated between skilfully twisting and turning his fingers and gently fucking Pierce with them. Pierce gasped. How could he have forgotten such a wonderful, intense sensation?

Noah kissed him again, invading more of his body and swallowing Pierce's moans. It felt marvellous. When Noah moved up the bed and fumbled with something, Pierce barely paid attention, completely focused on his own body.

The typical sounds of a condom wrapper being torn open and the snapping of a lube bottle's lid caught his attention. He really had to stop this. Any second now Noah would try to fuck him. It had been years since Pierce had bottomed for someone and he hadn't enjoyed it much, but the vague memories didn't compare with what he was experiencing now. When Noah's fingertip found and rubbed his magic spot, his brain's capacity to think was fried by the white-hot sparks those talented fingers sent up his spine. He was really going to do this, wasn't he? He was going to let Noah fuck him. Looking up at Noah, he tried to word his doubts. Instead, the raw need he saw in Noah's dark, lust-glazed eyes only added to his own explosive arousal.

"Ready for me, baby?" Noah's voice was a low, sexy purr and Pierce's body willingly gave him the answer he wanted.

A shifting of the mattress and Noah's wonderful fingers slipped out of Pierce, leaving him too empty and yearning for the fullness to return.

"Noah, please…" Pierce heard his own moan. It was an embarrassingly needy whimper.

"Please what, baby?" Noah teased him with the seductive tone of his voice as much as with the sweet pressure against his hole.

*What the hell…?*

"Please fuck me," Pierce begged. "I need you…in me—now!"

Noah's low chuckle turned into a growl as he entered Pierce in slow motion. Pierce knew Noah had prepared him well. The burn was minimal and was soon replaced by pure pleasure when Noah started moving, stroking Pierce's insides with his hard length. Lowering his head, Noah kissed him, gently at first then downright obscenely, fucking him both ends until he had to come up for air, panting heavily.

"Oh yeah, baby, this feels so good... Yeah, right—oh yes, yes, yes, oh, do that again!" Pierce knew he was babbling but he just couldn't make himself stop. It was all too much, too intense—and much too soon his body started shaking as fireworks went off in his nerve endings. For a moment, the world stopped turning and there was nothing but the weight of Noah's sweat-slicked body pressing down on him, shifting against him, and the sounds of Noah's heavy breathing and his groan as he found his release seconds after Pierce.

They remained motionless while slowly coming back down, arms and legs entangled, sticky bodies pressed together.

Eventually Noah shifted to pull out of Pierce's body. "Sorry, baby." He smiled when Pierce protested faintly and brushed a kiss on Pierce's lips before peeling off the condom and discarding it. "Let's rest a little, shall we?" Noah whispered and snaked an arm around Pierce's waist to pull him close, burying his face in Pierce's neck.

"Hmm," Pierce sighed contentedly, floating in a cloud of bliss.

It was pitch black outside when Pierce opened his eyes again. His chest was pressed to Noah's sleep-warmed back. He lifted his head to squint at the alarm clock on the nightstand. It was well past midnight and he wondered if he should go home. The faint light from the numbers on the clock was illuminating the smooth curve of Noah's bare shoulder in an eerie greenish shade. Pierce brushed his lips across the pale skin, tasting salt and feeling the heat of Noah's body. Before last night, he hadn't spent the night with a lover for more than a year and he'd always preferred to have his own space, but suddenly he just wanted to stay. Stay, sleep with Noah curled up in his arms and wake up and find him still there. He kissed Noah's shoulder again, inhaling the faint scent of soap and sweat that lingered on his skin. *I could get used to him being around,* he thought. It was a nice feeling. A little scary, but nice.

Noah shifted and grumbled in his sleep.

"Shhh." Pierce stroked Noah's shoulder gently.

"Huh?" Noah jerked awake. "What?"

"Nothing, sorry. I didn't mean to wake you up," Pierce soothed.

Noah looked around, confused and sleep-dazed. "I guess I...drifted off. Sorry." He yawned.

"I did too." Pierce smiled, lazily running his fingers over Noah's smooth back. "There really isn't an inch of you that isn't stunningly beautiful, is there?" He felt Noah's smile more than he saw it.

"You're a shameless flatterer," Noah scolded softly and rolled onto his back, shifting away from Pierce's touch.

"It's true, though. You've really got a gorgeous body." His hand trailed down the hard length of Noah's chest and stomach, drawing random little circles on the smooth skin. "And somehow it's fascinating to think that this body has fathered a child."

Noah snorted. "Yeah, well, fascinating may not be quite the right word for it."

"I think it is. I've never really thought about it, but it's amazing that something as wonderful as Phoebe exists only because of you. You made her — literally."

"Shit, Pierce, have you always been this sappy?" Noah laughed, sounding a little uncomfortable.

"No, not really. Sorry, I didn't mean to creep you out. It's just really..." He searched for the right word. "Awe-inspiring somehow, you know? I've never been with a guy who had a child before. At least not that I know of."

"It's not that big a deal."

"I think it is. Especially since you're the one who raises her. How did...? I hope you don't mind me asking, but how did it happen, anyway?"

"What do you mean?"

"Well, seeing as you're currently in bed with me, I'm having a bit of trouble understanding how Phoebe could come along. You obviously had sex with her mother, I understand that much. Do you play with both or did you play with girls before you found out that you like boys better?"

Noah tensed under Pierce's touch and gently removed his hand.

"I had a brief fling with Phoebe's egg donor, but apart from that I'm entirely gay."

"Why? Did you want to find out if girls were an alternative?" Pierce asked lightly.

"No. I just... I thought it was the right thing to be with her. It wasn't. We were young, inexperienced and she ended up pregnant."

"And how come Phoebe lives with you?"

"Well, someone had to take care of her." Noah shrugged off the question.

"True, but you'd expect the mother to raise her child."

"Maybe. But she didn't. Never wanted her. She had her and that was all."

"What about your parents? Did they help you?"

Noah frowned, clearly more than unwilling to answer the question. He sighed. "No. They kicked me out when they found out. I went to live with...a friend at university for a while and when Phoebe was born I took her in with me and moved to the single parent programme. It was quite funny 'cause I was the only guy there."

"I bet you could have had your pick." Pierce tried for a lighter tone. "There's nothing women like better than a guy who takes care of a baby, is there?"

Noah smirked. "Yeah, I still don't know who was more disappointed about my being gay — the girls or me."

"You must have had an awfully hard time with all that responsibility," Pierce said.

"I still don't know how it all worked back then, but somehow it did. My friend, David, was great. He helped me get a job at university so I could work from home and generally supported me a lot. Then Judith showed up and looked after Pheebs for a couple of hours a day and I could study some more and, well, somehow it worked. Does your family know?" Noah asked suddenly, swiftly changing the focus to Pierce.

"What? That I'm gay?"

"Uh-huh."

"Yes, they know."

"How was it for you when they found out?"

"I'm not sure when they found out exactly, to be honest. I remember realising that I found boys far more interesting than girls when I was about fifteen.

My parents never seemed to think anything about me telling them about the guys at school. When I eventually told my mum that I'd got my first kiss, she asked who it was. She smiled when I told her and said she'd thought so, since I seemed to be very smitten with him."

"She knew?"

"Apparently."

"And she didn't mind?"

"No, she was pretty cool about it. Nor did my dad, in fact. They were really easy about letting us spend time together. They even let us hang out in my room and all that."

"Huh? Well, I suppose there was no risk that either of you would end up pregnant," Noah said dryly.

"No, we didn't take any risks." Pierce smiled.

Noah looked at him earnestly. "We were using contraceptives, you know. I didn't really know much about it, since I'd never had to worry about any of that stuff, but I was aware of what could happen. I'm still not sure what exactly went wrong. I know I didn't use the condom correctly the first few times, but she said it didn't matter anyway since she was on the pill."

"Noah, don't blame yourself. It happens. And Phoebe is a wonderful result, no matter if she was planned or not."

"I know. I just wish her family would see it that way too."

"You're her family, sweetheart."

"You always have an answer, don't you?" Noah sounded annoyed.

"Maybe that's just because I'm a bit older than you and I have the luxury of seeing things from a little distance. Have you spoken to your parents since?"

"No," Noah said resolutely. "And I'm not going to. They made their point clear when they booted me out."

"But Phoebe is their grandchild," Pierce reminded him carefully.

"No, she's not. Not according to them."

"What? She's your daughter, so of course she is."

Noah shook his head sadly. "I wasn't married to her mother when she was conceived, so she's not a legal child. They might have ignored that if we'd at least got married afterwards, but since we didn't, they don't consider Phoebe to be related to them at all. Besides, they don't regard me as their son."

"Gosh, Noah, that's pretty pathetic. I don't even really know what to say, it's just too horrible. I didn't know people still thought like that."

"Oh, they do," Noah said flatly.

"Thanks for telling me, sweetheart. I just hope it doesn't mean you have to kill me now," he teased and poked Noah's side.

"Don't worry, I'll make it fast and easy for you."

"Hm, fast and easy can be quite nice, I suppose."

"What do you think of slow and intense, though?" Noah's voice dropped to that husky purr again that made Pierce's insides turn to jelly.

"I think if you do that I'll never get back home."

"Who said anything about you getting back home anyway?"

"Well, we didn't talk about it, but I figured…"

"What is it about you and leaving in the middle of the night?"

"Come on, Noah, you must know what it is about," Pierce answered sheepishly. "You don't just stay over uninvited."

"Well, sure, the basic rule of one-night stands. It's just... I don't really want you to leave right now. I've still got plans for you. *With* you."

"So you really want me to stay?" Pierce asked curiously.

"One thing about me, Pierce—if I say something, I mean it and I stick with it."

"I like that thing about you," Pierce whispered, nuzzling the short curls at the nape of Noah's neck.

Noah made a soft whimpering sound. "Basic rule of bringing up a child."

"Hmm, you're bringing up something else too." Pierce's hand slid down Noah's stomach to his stiffening cock and wrapped around it.

"Am I?" Noah gasped.

"I think we both are." Pierce rubbed his groin against Noah's hip while stroking him slowly.

"Oh, yeah, we are." He wasn't really surprised when Noah turned around in his arms and rolled him on his back, pushing up on top of him. The thought wasn't scary anymore.

Their lovemaking was lazy and unhurried, slowly coming down from the intense conversation earlier. They fell asleep again immediately afterwards, Noah curled up on his side, his back to Pierce as usual.

# Chapter Six

Pierce had overslept. Again. It seemed to be happening a lot to him lately. At least it wasn't quite as late as yesterday. He gingerly took stock of his body, relieved to find that he was fine apart from a slight, distinctive soreness. After a quick visit to the bathroom and an apologetic text message to his secretary, he went downstairs. Music drifted into the hall from behind the closed kitchen door, so Noah apparently hadn't left yet. When he opened the door, he couldn't help smiling at the scene. Noah was in the middle of the room, Phoebe's legs wrapped around his waist, and he was whirling her around to the song that was playing on the radio. Phoebe's little-girl giggles were almost drowning out the music. She was clearly loving it.

"Good morning, gorgeous!" Noah smiled when he spun around and discovered Pierce. A self-conscious expression appeared on his face as he stopped dancing and put Phoebe on her chair.

"Time to finish your breakfast now, pumpkin," he said softly and kissed the top of her head.

"Good morning back." Pierce stifled a yawn.

"Did you sleep well?" Noah turned to him, holding up a mug in a wordless offer.

"Yes, please." Pierce nodded. "I did. Much too well, to be honest. I don't usually lie in so late."

Noah raised an eyebrow meaningfully but refrained from reminding him that this was already the second time. "Don't worry. You probably needed it. Hungry?"

Bare-footed, unshaved and dressed in faded blue jeans and a smooth black T-shirt, Noah looked gloriously dishevelled and sexy. A satisfied sparkle lit up the blue ice of his eyes. Pierce swallowed nervously. Noah really shouldn't be allowed to look like that when minors were present. The thoughts those kiss-swollen lips inspired certainly wouldn't be admitted to the breakfast table.

"Not yet. Just coffee's fine."

Noah handed him a steaming mug and their fingers brushed as Pierce took it. Looking up, he met Noah's eyes. They mirrored his own confused feelings. Last night had been a revelation in many ways for Pierce and it had caught him entirely off guard. Now, most of all, he felt uncertain what to expect from Noah, who was struggling with his own emotions, judging by the silent storm that was raging in those blue depths. Unwillingly, Pierce dragged his eyes away from Noah's face and found himself looking straight into the younger version. Phoebe.

She watched him in bewilderment, the bright blue eyes that were so much like her father's darting back and forth between Noah's and Pierce's faces.

"Good morning, Phoebe," Pierce greeted uncertainly.

"Good morning," Phoebe answered in her high-pitched voice and continued shovelling breakfast cereal into her mouth.

"Did you sleep well?" Pierce enquired politely.

She nodded earnestly. "Uh-huh. Did you sleep with Daddy?" she asked innocently, making Pierce gasp and sputter into his coffee.

"He slept *over*, pumpkin," Noah clarified carefully, a smile tugging at his eyes.

"In your bed?"

The colour drained from Noah's face but he answered truthfully, if reluctantly. "Yes."

Her attention shifted to Pierce. "Did you kiss Daddy?"

"Um..." Pierce shot Noah a helpless glance. Noah winced, but stuck with the truth. "Yes. We kissed."

Phoebe took a moment to process that information, chewing her cereal thoughtfully before she looked at Pierce again. "Are you Daddy's boyfriend now?"

Pierce watched the colour blossom on Noah's face as he racked his brain for an answer but was saved by Noah, who took the fire for him again. "What makes you think he's my boyfriend?"

"Well, Anna said her sister slept with Frank and kissed him and that he is now her boyfriend." She shoved another spoonful of cereal into her mouth.

Noah watched her crunch for a moment. "What would you think of him being my boyfriend?"

She shrugged. "It's nice to have a friend." Pierce's heart hammered madly against his ribs as his eyes met Noah's. That little girl made it all sound so simple.

"Will he and June live with us?"

Noah took a deep breath before he answered. "Easy, Pheebs. We haven't really talked about any of that yet, you know," he said carefully. "Sometimes these things just aren't that simple."

Pierce crossed the short distance between them. He would have loved to put his arms around Noah but didn't know how much physical intimacy Noah would deem suitable in Phoebe's presence, so he settled for just brushing the back of his finger against Noah's hip in a silent supportive gesture.

"But maybe sometimes they can be that simple." He hoped desperately that Noah understood what he was trying to say. He wanted Noah, and he wanted him for more than just a sexy night. The realisation made him giddy and a little sick with nerves. "Don't you think?"

"That's…uh, I…um…" Noah's voice was strangled. He looked overwhelmed and at a loss for words as he kept staring at Pierce.

"You don't have to decide just now," Pierce whispered softly.

Noah stared at him with wide, slightly terrified eyes. "The thing is… I think I like the idea," he said quietly.

"Really?"

"Yeah. It's scary, though." Noah leaned in to kiss Pierce. A shy, chaste kiss that was over much too fast. It wasn't quite what Pierce was longing for, but it would have to do.

Noah took a breath to say something more but the ringing of the doorbell interrupted him.

"Sally!" Phoebe shrieked and jumped up, bouncing to the door excitedly. Noah went after her and struggled with her briefly to make her put on her coat. Then he gave her a quick peck on the cheek and she was gone, wonderfully oblivious of the confusion she had bestowed upon the two adults.

"She's quite something," Pierce said after a moment.

Noah sighed and nodded. "Yeah, she is. Gosh, I didn't think it would be so weird explaining to her...about you."

"She didn't seem to mind me being around much."

Noah looked at him sceptically. "She hasn't processed it yet, I guess. She doesn't know what it means, since she's never seen me with anyone."

"You've really never brought anyone home?"

"Nope."

"But... I mean, you have been with someone since you've had her, right?"

Noah smirked. "I haven't had a steady lover since she was three, which she doesn't remember. Since then, I just...well, it was always their place and it never went beyond seeing each other a couple of times."

"I guess being a single dad doesn't make dating any easier, huh?"

"No, it doesn't." Noah took a breath and frowned. "You see, I don't want to put her through seeing me with a lot of different guys, so I don't want her to meet the ones that I'm not going to get steady with anyway. And so far, well, there just hasn't been anyone."

"What do you think she'll make of...?" He searched for the right word. "...This?" Somehow 'us' seemed too early and too presumptuous.

"I don't know, Pierce." Noah's frown deepened. "I really don't. To be honest, I don't even know what this is yet. I... It's nice to be with you but...I'm just not sure where this is going."

"Neither am I. But I'm willing to find out, you know?" Pierce said softly, snaking an arm around Noah's waist.

Noah stared at him with those intense, haunted eyes. "I just don't know if I can do this. It's... My life is pretty complicated as it is. It wouldn't be fair if I let you get into something and…" he broke off, looking scared and very, very young.

Pierce raised his arm and cupped Noah's face with one hand, stroking his stubbly chin soothingly with his thumb. "The truth is, Noah, I already am in this. I don't know why, but you've got to me fast and deep. I'd like to try this with you and see where it takes us."

He watched Noah worry his bottom lip with his teeth in distress. There was obviously something he didn't know how to say but needed to get out.

"I know how important Phoebe is for you, sweetheart. She's your priority, and I accept that. I'm not asking for a guarantee, either. I know it's still early and we'll just have to see how it works out."

Noah stared at him silently for a long moment. When he finally spoke, his voice was rough with emotion. "Phoebe needs me. She really does, and she needs me a lot. More than you might think. There will be times when she…when you'll feel neglected because I have to take care of her. Do you really think you're going to be okay with that?"

"I want you, Noah. And Phoebe's gorgeous. I don't consider her a burden, if that's what you're worried about."

Noah let out a sad, frustrated chuckle. "I know how it goes, Pierce. I've been there before. There are certain limitations when you have a child. I can't just go out to dinner or the cinema or whatever when I want to. I can't just stay over at your place or go away for the weekend. My life's pretty boring in that respect and it's not going to change much for the next couple of years."

"I'm aware of that, but don't underestimate me, Noah. I want you and, even though I don't understand what it's like to be responsible for a child, to me, Phoebe is a part of you. A part I'd never ask or expect you to give up for me. Besides, other couples have children too," he finished lightly.

"Yes, but Phoebe is *my* child. She isn't yours and, frankly, I don't think you understand what it's like to be responsible for a child," Noah snapped, suddenly defensive. "You don't know how it feels to know that you're all that stands between this vulnerable little person and…" He broke off with an irritable huff.

"No, you're right, I don't," Pierce confirmed softly, pulling a reluctant Noah into his arms. "But I'm willing to find out. Noah, you're so used to being the one who's responsible that you're forgetting that you might need someone to take care of you too. I understand it's not an easy situation for you, but maybe you're asking a little too much of yourself. You give Phoebe everything she could ask for. Maybe you should learn to take a little for yourself too."

"I don't think I even know how that works anymore," Noah sighed.

"I know," Pierce whispered. "And I'd really like to show you."

"But…"

"Don't 'but' me, Noah." Pierce cut him off. "You deserve love and affection as much as anybody else. Don't deny yourself that."

Noah smiled slowly, resignedly. "You're really a raging romantic, aren't you?"

"Oh, the things you do to me, pretty baby." Pierce grinned and kissed him, delighted when Noah actually opened up and admitted him into his mouth.

"Hmm," Noah purred. "I think I know what you mean." There was a mischievous glitter in his eyes. "Do you have to go to work today?"

"Well, I already sent my secretary a message that I'd be late. Why?"

"Oh, I'm just thinking—I don't have to start any time soon."

"What exactly are you suggesting here?"

Noah's eyes darkened. "It's my home office day today, so I'll have to do some work at my desk and maybe you could…add to what's already on it."

"Sweetheart, you've got a one-track mind," Pierce scolded softly, following Noah to his office with a smile on his face.

Noah had them both undressed and Pierce draped across his desk in less than two minutes. Within another few minutes, they were both panting and sweating, desperate to find their release. It was uncomfortable, inelegant and extremely satisfying.

"Fancy meeting for dinner sometime this week?" Pierce asked when they'd dressed afterwards. He didn't like having to ask, but he really wanted to see Noah again as soon as possible. Most of all, he would have liked to take Noah out somewhere nice but knew Phoebe couldn't stay alone. Inviting himself to dinner at Noah's bordered on impoliteness, but he needed to set a date.

"Uh, I'm pretty busy this week, actually," Noah said hesitantly. "I suppose you could come around Friday night if you want."

Pierce let out a sigh. "Sorry, darling. Friday is family night. I promised my parents to join them for dinner." He thought for a moment. "You could come with me, you know," he suggested cautiously.

Noah looked panicky. "I've got to be home with Phoebe," he reminded.

"Besides, you think it's too early to meet my parents yet," Pierce finished for him.

"I'm afraid so, yes," Noah admitted. "I'm not good with parents."

"Don't worry. That can wait. We'll get there in your own sweet time." Pierce gave Noah a tender kiss. "You really taste nice. I'd be happy to meet you for dinner on Saturday, though."

Noah smiled. "Saturday it is. Six too early for you? That's our usual dinnertime, you know."

"I'll make it," Pierce promised.

Noah turned to the second table. "By the way, here's your laptop."

"Does it work again?"

A frown fluttered across Noah's face. "Of course."

"What was wrong with it?"

"A virus, as suspected. Fortunately it didn't do any serious damage—it was just a pain to get rid of. I installed a different programme that should keep stuff like that out of your system, hope you don't mind."

"No, not at all. Thanks. Um, Noah," Pierce started hesitantly.

"Yeah?"

"What exactly do you do as a job?"

"Computer consulting."

"Do you work for a company?"

"Nope, I'm a freelancer. The social scheme sucks but I get to choose the hours. Mostly, that is."

"Would you like to work for a company?"

"Depends." Noah sounded sceptical.

"On what?"

"On working hours. They'd have to be flexible enough for me to put Phoebe in. Payment of course. Distance to work, I guess. Why?"

"Oh, I was just thinking. There will be a job opening in IT at my company sometime soon and I'm sure your application would be appreciated."

Noah looked unconvinced. "I'll think about it."

"Okay." He took a small metal box from his laptop case and handed Noah a business card. "This is the company. If you're interested, just call and talk to Ms Foster. She can tell you what papers are required." He sighed. "I guess I should go now."

Noah's eyes met his and their gazes locked for a long moment. "Okay. I'll see you on Saturday then, baby. Take care," Noah said hoarsely and leaned in for a long, tender kiss goodbye.

# Chapter Seven

Trying to shake off an unsettling sense of apprehension, Pierce checked his watch for what felt like the hundredth time. The sad truth was he was not at all sure if Noah was going to turn up, which made him nervous and worried. The even sadder truth was he didn't know where recent events had left him standing with Noah. Even though he had encouraged it, he had been pleasantly surprised when his secretary had told him that Noah had indeed applied for the position in IT. The papers he had handed in were rather impressive, even more so considering he'd had to work and raise a child while studying. Noah had obviously been a top student and was exactly what they were looking for. The head of the personnel department had been over the moon with him and the interview had gone extremely well—up until the moment when Pierce had joined them, revealing that he was both the managing director and the owner of the company. That hadn't gone down well at all with Noah. In fact, he had been thoroughly pissed off and had wanted to retract his application altogether, leaving poor Ms Foster confused and disappointed until Pierce had managed to persuade him to at least think about it before calling it off.

After several days of silence, Noah had reluctantly agreed to meet him and talk about it in a more private setting. Pierce still didn't know what exactly had raised Noah's hackles, but he hoped they could sort it out. Losing Noah because of what had seemed an ideal arrangement for both of them would be unbearable.

At last he saw Noah approaching, following the waiter to Pierce's table. Watching more than one head turn in Noah's wake, Pierce felt a sense of pride chase away some of the concern inside him. He wanted Noah in his life, he was certain of that, and he wanted more than the few hours they got to spend together every week. After just one month, their relationship was still only delicately blossoming. In fact, they hadn't even declared it a relationship officially yet and the clash over Noah's job application that had led to almost a week of no contact other than a brief phone call had left Pierce dreading the worst.

"You look gorgeous," he greeted softly as Noah took a seat.

"Thank you." Noah looked a little self-conscious. He was dressed slightly less formally than the restaurant's usual clientele in figure-hugging black jeans, a shirt and suit jacket but he was handsome enough to get away with it and look fashionably casual rather than underdressed.

"What would you like to drink?"

"Just water."

"Can't I tempt you with a glass of this wonderful red wine?"

"No thanks, I'll stick with water."

"What is it with you and water?" Pierce teased.

"Nothing in particular, it's just that I don't drink much alcohol."

"Don't you like it?"

Noah shook his head. "More like I prefer to be sober in case Phoebe needs me."

Pierce waited until the waiter had handed Noah the menu and shuffled off to get his drink. "How are you?"

"Good, thanks."

"I'm glad you came," Pierce said quietly. Heaving a sigh, Noah looked at him with an accusing stare. "Yeah, well, I guess you're right. We should talk." A shudder ran down Pierce's spine at the chilly tone in Noah's voice.

"Why are you mad at me?"

Noah seemed to need a moment to think about his answer — or maybe he was just surprised at the direct question. "I'm not mad at you," he replied at last, sounding resigned.

"Funny how it looks suspiciously like you are, though."

"I'm not," Noah insisted. "I'm just…disappointed."

"Disappointed? Why would you be disappointed? Hell, all I did was offer you a job."

Waiting until the waiter had disappeared again after delivering his drink, Noah looked at him thoughtfully. "Because I didn't think it would be that way."

"What would be what way? I'm not following you."

Noah took a sip of his water and looked up defiantly. "Pierce, I understand that your income is several times higher than mine, but that doesn't mean you have to support me. I might not earn that much, but I'm coping. There is no need to make me a charity case."

"I'm not making you a charity case, Noah. What makes you even think that?"

"You offering me a job at your company, obviously."

"Fuck, Noah, I didn't offer you that job out of pity. You solved a problem my so-called specialist couldn't and I just thought you might be the right guy for the job. I was thinking about filling a position at my company mostly, to be honest. You being the one to fill it would be merely a nice side effect."

Noah waited quietly for the waiter to bring their food and leave. His voice was calm when he finally spoke. "So, asking me to apply for that position had nothing to do with the fact that I had my dick up your arse?"

Pierce managed not to sputter in his drink. "Hell, Noah. You can't just say things like that!"

"Why not? We're adults. We should talk like adults."

"Fine. No, the fact that we both had our dicks up our respective arses had nothing to do with that." The reminder hadn't strictly been necessary, but he just couldn't resist it. "Why do you think I let my personnel manager do the interview without me? I wanted her opinion on you first—a more objective opinion than mine—and I can assure you I wouldn't have asked you to work for me if she hadn't been convinced of your abilities."

"But you're the one who decides if I get to work for you or not."

Catching the emphasis, Pierce understood at last what Noah's real problem was and let out a sigh. "Not for me. I want you to work for my company, but not because you're my...lover or because of some odd sense of duty towards a single parent. There's a job opening at my company that needs to be filled and you just happen to be the right guy for it." He leaned in a little closer. "I want you in that position because I think you're good at it, Noah." He grinned, trying to ease some of the tension between them. "Not that I don't want to have you in a lot of other positions as my lover, but I'm enough of a businessman not to let my personal affection for you interfere with our working relationship."

"Do you really think separating the two can work?" Noah asked sceptically. "What if there is something wrong at work, say we disagree about something, or say I mess up? How would you react?"

"The same as with everyone. I'd talk to you about it, sort it out or rather have you sort it out and that would be it. I wouldn't take it to a personal level."

Noah seemed to consider his answer before asking the next question. "What if we have a fight? A good old domestic, in the morning, right before we go to work? How would you react if you met me in the office an hour later and I told you that the main server had crashed and there wouldn't be any email traffic for at least three hours?"

Pierce couldn't help smiling. "You have a vivid imagination, my dear." The serious expression on Noah's face sobered him up quickly. "I can see your point and I admit it's not a scenario I'd be happy with. However, I don't tend to take those kinds of problems out on my employees, so in a situation like this I'd probably be pissed off with you on the personal level while asking you to do your job and sort the mess out on the professional level. In the evening, I'd probably talk to my boyfriend about our crap days at work but I wouldn't make my IT manager suffer because my lover's thrown a strop. Think you could live with that?"

Noah took a long time to choose his next bite, chew and swallow, before washing it down with some water.

"This is not the real problem, though, is it?" Pierce asked softly.

"It's part of the problem," Noah said miserably. "You see, it's all sort of mingled." He took a deep breath and released it on a long sigh. "When we started...seeing each other, I wasn't exactly looking for something serious, I guess you know that."

"You don't always have to look to find something," Pierce said warily. The conversation was going into the entirely wrong direction.

Noah sighed again and rubbed his forehead. "No, but you'd actually have to... Look, after those first two nights, things just kind of developed a dynamic of their own."

"Are you saying you're not happy with what happened between us?"

"That's not the point."

"What is the point?"

"The point is I'm not ready for it. I can't give you what you want from me. I just can't be what you want."

A hollow, humourless chuckle found its way out of Pierce's throat. "And what would that be?"

"You're obviously looking for something far more serious than what I had in mind. I told you that my daughter is the top priority in my life."

"And who do you think you'd have to be for me?"

Noah looked at him for a moment. "You want someone you can keep," he said simply. "In every meaning of the word. I'm not material for a kept boy and I can't promise you that what's between us is going to last, either. I've got too much on my plate already for yet another commitment."

"Has it occurred to you that I've no intention of becoming another obligation in your life?" Pierce raised his hands in a helpless gesture. "Screw it, Noah. I want us to be lovers and friends, but above all, partners. That includes both of us giving something to the other and receiving something in return. If by a kept boy you mean that I'd pay for you to be my lover, you're completely wrong. I wouldn't do that and I can't believe you're even thinking along those lines. I know you've worked hard and you have my respect for what you have achieved. I'm well aware that I have more money, but I'm also aware of the fact that you don't need me to help you out financially.

"You are right, though. I do want to keep you. I want to keep you close as my boyfriend, as my partner. What I want from you is simply to spend time with you, go out, take Phoebe and June to the park maybe and fuck you senseless afterwards. Phoebe's got a wonderful father, but you're more than that and that's who I want. I don't want to be another obligation for you, Noah—I simply want to be with the wonderful man you are." Reaching across the table, he covered Noah's fingers with his own, relieved when Noah didn't pull away. "Don't just run away, please. At least give us a try."

Toying absently with his food, Noah made him wait for an answer. When he finally looked up, there was the faint crease of a frown between his eyebrows. "I'm not going to take that job, Pierce. If you want me to fill that position, I'd be happy for contracted work as your consultant, but I'll remain freelance. We'd have to sort out the details, but the costs for you shouldn't be any higher than what you'd have to pay if you employed me. I know it's not what you want, but I've worked too hard to establish my business to abandon it for a potentially temporary employment."

"Potentially temporary?" Pierce echoed, annoyed by the insinuation. "I'm not the kind of employer who replaces employees at the spur of a moment. Not as long as they're good, anyway, you know."

Noah shrugged but his expression remained set. "No offence, Pierce. I prefer to remain independent and I like to know where I'm standing. It's only fair if you know it too."

"Are we still talking about that job offer?" Pierce asked.

Noah took a sip of water before he answered. "As for the private part..." he broke off with a sigh. "I like being with you. A lot. But I can't promise you anything. We can keep seeing each other when we both have the time and see where it takes us, but that's all I can give you at the moment."

His even and still business-like tone cut into Pierce's heart. Noah could have been discussing the weather for all the passion he showed at what would be their future. "That's all I'm going to get, isn't it?" Pierce asked, forcing himself to sound just as strictly professional. Noah nodded wordlessly.

"Fine. As far as the job's concerned, set up a contract you're comfortable with and send it to me. I'll have my lawyer look into it, but I'm sure we'll reach an agreement. About us... When you say we can keep seeing each other, where exactly does that leave us?"

A faint smile pulled up the corners of Noah's mouth. "I guess that leaves us where we spend time together, go out and to the park and I fuck you senseless afterwards."

"Sure you're okay with that?"

"Uh-huh." Noah nodded.

"So just to let me get this straight and make sure we both know where we're standing—you're going to do IT consultancy for my company and we're officially dating?" *Gosh, that makes us sound like we're teenagers,* Pierce thought irritably.

"That sums it up quite well," Noah said lightly.

"Okay." Pierce nodded slowly, wondering how Noah would react to his next question. "Just in case the matter comes up... How do you want me to refer to you?"

"I think Noah is quite all right," Noah deadpanned.

Pierce rolled his eyes. "You know what I mean."

Noah sighed and turned serious. "Yes, I know. How about *the guy I'm dating*?" he offered.

"If that's what you want. It's your title, after all," Pierce said lightly, trying not to show his hurt. Noah looked at him thoughtfully. "What did you have in mind?"

"I was more thinking along the lines of partner," Pierce suggested hopefully.

Not unexpectedly, Noah shook his head.

"No?" Pierce asked.

"No." Noah held his gaze and smiled softly. "No, but I'll meet you halfway."

"Halfway? Now where does that leave us?"

"That leaves us where you call me your boyfriend."

Somehow Pierce just couldn't be bothered to care about the heads that turned when he leaned across the table to pull Noah into a long, deep kiss.

# Chapter Eight

"Fuck, I don't think I can move anymore." Noah panted and settled on his side.

"Then don't. It's probably safer for my virtue anyway."

Noah chuckled. "I didn't know you were worried about your virtue," he teased, stroking Pierce's side with his hand.

"I'm not. But your fingers are really the meanest incorporation of evil I've ever come across."

"Are they? You seem to have led a sheltered life, my dear."

"I haven't. Not at all. I bet there's a lot I could show you."

"Really? You want to show me stuff? Such as?"

"Don't know yet. But you would be surprised." He'd meant it as a joke, but something inside Pierce's contented, well-fucked brain clicked and he remembered the first time he had met Noah. Vividly and in colourful detail. Noah collared and on a leash. Trying to get away from the stinging bite of the nipple clamps. Not getting hard when Pierce fucked him.

Robert shooting his load all over... He really didn't need *that* picture.

"Noah?"

"Yeah?"

"Are you really into the scene?"

"What scene?" A sleepy murmur.

"BDSM."

"What makes you — oh." Noah's body went rigid.

"It's okay if you are," Pierce said quickly.

"Well, I'm not," Noah answered in a tight voice. "What about you?"

"Me?"

"Yes. What were you doing at the club? At first I thought you were one of the Doms, but you don't really seem to be one."

"Oh, I see. I'm not a Dom," Pierce explained. "I just go to the club sometimes. It's...well, it's a good place to meet people."

"For sex," Noah finished with a knowing look.

"Yes, for sex," Pierce admitted, a little embarrassed. "I haven't had a proper relationship in ages and sometimes...you know."

"You just want to get laid." Noah grinned. "Sounds familiar."

"Well, it's nice to do it with not just your own hand every now and then," Pierce said apologetically.

Shrugging, Noah raised his hands. "Hey, no need to tell me."

"No, probably not. I suppose it's the same for you, basically. It's not really what I want though. I'm a one-man guy essentially."

"Are you?"

Pierce nodded earnestly, watching Noah's expression as he spoke. "Absolutely. Mr Right, marriage, a family — the whole package. I've always wanted that." *And maybe I've found Mr Right at last,* he added silently.

Noah laughed, seemingly oblivious to the deeper meaning in Pierce's words. "Gosh, baby, if I hadn't already checked every inch of you, I'd say there's a little girl hiding in there somewhere."

"Maybe there is, I can't help it." Pierce smiled.

"Do you really want a family?" Noah sounded sceptical.

"Sure. The hardest part about finding out I'm gay was accepting that I'll probably never have children of my own."

"Oh."

"So you see, for me, being with someone who already has a child is the perfect solution."

Knowing that Noah had a hard enough time committing to their relationship as it was, Pierce didn't want to push him any further just yet. "Anyway, when I go out, I hate wasting the best part of an evening trying to find that one guy who isn't a complete waste of space. At the club I know that at least the clientele is decent."

"Decent," Noah chuckled. "Not quite the word most people would use to describe the members of a leather club."

Pierce grinned and rolled his eyes. "You know what I mean. The guys there are okay — no loonies and they respect certain rules."

"Good territory for hunting, huh?" Noah smirked.

"It is, actually."

"So which ones do you go for? Doms or subs?"

"Both, actually, although I don't really play their games. I'm pretty...moderate as you probably noticed."

"Uh-huh, compared to some of the stuff they do there, you are. So far, that is," he added gravely. Picking up on the undertone in Noah's voice, Pierce realised that the last four words contained both a question and a warning.

"I'm not into whipping or bondage, Noah," he said softly. "And I certainly wouldn't ask you to do anything you're not entirely comfortable with."

Noah looked at him guardedly. "But there are a few things you would like to do, I suppose."

"Well, yes."

Noah nodded slowly. "What exactly?"

"Nothing specific, but I like toys and you'd look lovely tied up and blindfolded." Lovely was an understatement for the image in Pierce's head. He quickly shoved it aside when he saw the expression on Noah's face. It bordered on disgust.

"Not your thing?" he asked.

"That's never gonna happen," Noah muttered through clenched teeth.

"Okay," Pierce soothed. "As I said, I wouldn't ask for anything you don't want."

"Good."

"One question though. If you don't like toys and ties, then what was that thing with Robert about?"

Noah flinched at the mention of Robert's name and answered very quietly. "Don't go there." It could be a plea or a warning, but the vehemence was written all over Noah's face. He had gone pale and looked faintly sick.

"Easy, Noah. No need to bite my head off. I was just wondering because... I never had you down as the submissive type in the first place and, well, the way you are with me—you're pretty...intense." He

97

swallowed. "You're always totally in charge. You're really more of a Dom than a sub, aren't you?"

Noah sighed and rubbed his eyes. "I wasn't kidding that first night when I told you that I always top—I do."

"So I noticed. That is, you do now, but you didn't..." Pierce started, but Noah cut him off.

"I always bottomed for the first two guys I was with, okay? Then I met Phoebe's egg donor, and I obviously topped her, if that's what you want to call it. I let David top me a couple of times after that, but ever since then I've preferred topping."

"But you still bottomed for... Robert. And me, on that occasion. You even submitted," Pierce reminded him, shuddering at the memory of that particular night.

"That was...an exception. I don't bottom, I'm not a sub and I'm not into the scene. Not at all," Noah snapped, his tone a warning not to dig any further.

"And you're not keen on pain either, right?" Pierce asked guardedly, choosing to ignore the warning.

"No, I'm not. I enjoy a rough fuck as much as the next guy, but that's about it."

"Then what was that thing with Robert about?" Pierce knew he was treading a fine line, but he needed to ask anyway. "I'd like to know what happened with him, Noah. I don't want to push for answers, but it's obvious that something went terribly wrong between the two of you. Don't you think talking about it would make it easier for you to get over it?"

Avoiding his eyes, Noah said in a tight voice, "I don't want that topic to ever come up, but thanks for the offer."

Pierce watched him for a long moment. Noah's reaction only confirmed his assumption, or rather dread. It was clear that something bad had happened to Noah, but it was also clear that Noah wasn't going to talk about it of his own will, so Pierce decided to push him a bit more. "Were you just curious?"

Noah groaned. "Look, it was just something I had to do, okay?"

Pierce didn't miss Noah's exact wording. "Had to do? Why?"

"Because...it just happened. Leave it at that, will you?"

"Fuck, Noah, I was there. I saw what he did to you. He hurt you and abused you. Why didn't you stop him?"

"I couldn't." Noah sounded strangled.

"Why not? There were rules, weren't there? You could have just used your safe words and made him stop."

"I couldn't."

"I know Robert's a bastard, Noah, but I've never heard of him continuing when a sub safe worded."

"I didn't, though."

"What?"

"I didn't safe word," Noah explained quietly.

Pierce was stunned. "What do you mean, you didn't?"

"I never used any of my safe words."

"But...why not? For fuck's sake, Noah, he whipped you and if you really hate bottoming as much as you say, then he basically raped you too!" Pierce shouted. "He's one of the most sadistic Doms and you're not a masochist. Why did you take it?"

"Because he paid me for it." The words seemed to choke Noah.

"For...for what exactly?"

"To let him treat me as his sub."

"He paid you for it," Pierce repeated quietly. "That's an awful way to make money."

"Don't fucking judge me," Noah hissed defensively.

"I'm not, but honestly, I don't really know what to think of this right now. He paid you to be his sub and he didn't allow you to use your safe words?" Pierce was trying hard to suppress his anger. That was inexcusable and, if it was true, he'd make sure Robert's reputation in the scene would be destroyed.

"No. No, I could have used them. But part of the deal was that if I used more than just the warning, I'd get only half of the money."

"Why didn't you at least use the warning then?" What was it? Butterfly. And stop was...pumpkin. Noah's nickname for Phoebe. *No, please.*

"It had something to do with Phoebe, didn't it?" Pierce asked quietly, horrified. The thought of Noah being forced into something so appalling by fear for his child sent a shudder down his spine.

Noah took his time to answer. When he did, his voice was carefully controlled but the emotions kept seeping through. "Phoebe's got a congenital heart defect. The doctors found out shortly after she was born, but there wasn't much they could do about it other than give her medication to...keep her going. The only permanent solution is surgery, but no one has dared do it yet, because she's an extremely complicated case and the risk of...losing her is just too high."

"I... I don't know what to say, Noah. This is just horrible. Is there really nothing that can be done? What about transplantation?"

"No," Noah whispered hollowly and took a breath. "Transplantation is nearly impossible. She's got an extremely rare blood group, courtesy of me. The chances of finding a suitable donor are less than zero, especially since it started getting worse at the beginning of last year. She's growing and that adds to the strain on her heart. The only possibility is a new surgery method in the States. They have developed a technique for cases like Phoebe's and have already performed three surgeries successfully. It's still considered a high-risk treatment, but it's the only chance she's got. It's either that or…continuing to watch her die, day by day, so I decided to have the surgery done. Problem is, it's a pioneering technique and not available on the NHS, so I'll have to come up with the money for everything myself. I…I've been trying to save money for ages, just in case, but I just couldn't come up with the kind of money it takes and Phoebe doesn't have much time left, so when I met Robert and he offered me even more than what she needed, I just…I accepted."

"So you did this all for Phoebe? It's why you chose her nickname as the word to stop him, isn't it?"

"Yeah. So I'd think of her if I was tempted to use it and remember to go through with it." He looked up sadly. "I just couldn't let her down, Pierce."

Pierce needed a moment to digest this information before he could speak. "Oh God, Noah. I don't know what to say. I'm so, so sorry, sweetheart. Taking advantage of you like that—it's unforgivable. I never would have touched you if I'd known…"

"It's okay," Noah whispered hoarsely. "You didn't know it."

"Yes, but still. I feel horrible about this."

Noah let out a bitter chuckle. "If it's any consolation, what happened with you wasn't the worst part of it. I was only two weeks into it then and he was still mostly teaching me how he wanted me to behave."

"You achieved such a level of control after only two weeks of training? That's really quite impressive."

"Thank you," Noah said dryly. "I was highly motivated."

"I'm sorry, that was inconsiderate of me," Pierce apologised. "But, seriously, I've seen a couple of subs and you were good. You really had me believe you were into it."

"Had I? You noticed that I wasn't, well, enthusiastic," Noah reminded him.

"Oh, that." Pierce smiled. "Well, in my experience it's not at all uncommon for a sub not to be fully aroused during sex. For them, serving their Master is more important than their own pleasure."

"Yeah, I remember that line," Noah grumbled.

"I thought you wanted it harder, but hurting a guy in bed is just really not my thing."

Noah nodded slowly. "I noticed. You were trying to be careful with me. I did appreciate it, you know, and I might have actually enjoyed it if that sick fuck hadn't been watching."

"Really?" Pierce asked, surprised. "Even though you bottomed?"

Noah gave a shrug. "I prefer topping now, but I used to quite like it," he answered miserably.

"But you don't anymore, do you?"

Noah swallowed and silently shook his head. Pierce gently wrapped his arms around Noah's shoulders, relieved when Noah leaned into the hug with a tired sigh. He understood that opening up to him like that hadn't been easy for Noah and decided to give him a break. "About Phoebe...is there anything I can do?"

"No."

"When's the operation due?"

"Not until after her birthday in June. They want her to grow some more and put on some weight so her body has more reserves."

"What's going to happen?"

"I'm going to take her to the States for about two weeks and...hope for the best."

"Why didn't you tell me before?"

"It's just not something you go around and tell other people, you know?" Noah said irritably and tried to pull out of Pierce's embrace, but Pierce held on to him.

"But I'm not other people, darling," he whispered into the soft curls behind Noah's ear. "I'm here for you and you can tell me things. That's the way it works when you're a couple, you know?" He felt Noah nod. "Do you want me to go with you?" he asked quietly after a long time of simply holding Noah tight.

"Would you?" Noah sounded as if the possibility hadn't even occurred to him.

"Sure. If you want me there, I'll be there. Just say the word."

"I'm not sure, to be honest. I think I'd like you to be there but I... I just don't know what's going to happen and... I can't stand thinking that maybe..." he broke off with a heartbreaking sob. "She could die there, Pierce. And if she does, it's my fault, because I decided to have it done. I — I'm not ready for that. I c-can't l-lose her," Noah stammered through a series of barely suppressed sobs, finally giving in to his pain.

"I know. But you're right, it's the best chance she's got. You've got to take it, Noah. I'll go with you, okay? I'm not leaving you to deal with this on your own."

Pierce felt like screaming himself. He wanted to rant and rave, shout and break things. The injustice of it all made him fume with rage inside. Noah was still so young and hadn't ever done anything wrong to deserve this but life just seemed to keep dealing him the worst blows it could come up with.

His parents had abandoned him and the child he'd fathered. Noah had done all in his power to protect and raise that child, but a cruel twist of fate threatened to take her away from him anyhow. Then Robert had taken advantage of Noah's situation and bought him to abuse his body as much as his mind. And there was nothing he could do. Pierce suppressed his anger as best he could and held on to Noah, kept stroking him in the silent promise to be there and support him.

# Chapter Nine

Pierce was uncomfortably aware of a lot of curious pairs of eyes resting on him and following him as he made his way through the club. Some of the men present greeted him with a brief nod and a smile. Others, who didn't know him, just stared at him, trying to size him up. He didn't bother with any of them. Instead, he gave the bartender a signal and went to find a table in a quiet corner.

"Hello, Pierce. Good to see you."

"Hello, Francis. Thanks for making time for me."

Francis grinned broadly and gathered Pierce into a tight hug. "Quit the show, little bro. How are you? Haven't seen you around here for ages. I started thinking you might not like the location anymore. Or is it just me?"

Pierce chuckled. "Stop being stupid. I just...have been a little preoccupied lately."

Francis made a soft humming sound. "And does your preoccupation have a name, too?"

Pierce grinned. "Noah."

"Noah. Nice name." Francis looked at him intently for a moment. "You're serious about him, aren't you?"

"I think I've fallen in love with him."

"Ooh, nice one. The L-word at last. Tell me more. Are you here to ask me to be your best man at the wedding?"

"Not quite. Thanks." He smiled at the waiter who set their drinks on the table and picked up his glass.

"What's the problem?" Francis had always been very straightforward. He believed in talking things out and finding a solution before they had the chance to become a problem.

"What makes you think there is a problem?" Pierce asked nervously. Francis also had the uncanny ability to read most people like open books.

"You sitting here all fidgety and anxious while you're telling me you're in love. Go ahead, tell me about him."

"Sometimes I think you really are a psychic, France," Pierce joked feebly.

"I'm just paying attention." Francis leant back in his chair, his body relaxed and open. He had also always been an extremely good listener.

Pierce took a breath. "It's…Noah. I love him and I'm pretty sure he has feelings for me too. I've been seeing him for almost four months now and generally it's working quite well, I think, although…" He sighed. "Well, he keeps me at a distance and I think he doesn't trust me."

"Knowing you, I suppose he doesn't have a reason not to trust you, right?"

"It's not that. I don't think he worries too much about me cheating on him. He wouldn't put up with it, I guess, but he isn't the jealous type." He gulped down some of his drink, trying to find the right words to explain his thoughts.

"Noah's just so... He doesn't let me take charge. Ever. He's got a daughter, Phoebe. She's six and the most gorgeous little creature I've ever seen. He was only nineteen when she was born and he's looked after her ever since. He's great with her. I respect that she's his child and he gets to make the decisions about her upbringing, but somehow it's like...he's trying to take care of me too. Like he doesn't always realise that I'm an adult and very capable of making my own decisions. At first I thought that maybe, given some time, he'd come to understand that he doesn't have to look after me, but I don't think he will."

"Have you talked to him about it?"

"Yes, of course. Talked — and fought. Repeatedly."

"What does he say?"

"That he isn't trying to boss me around but that Phoebe is his responsibility, so he has to set the rules when the three of us are together."

"He does have a point there," Francis said thoughtfully. "What's it like when it's just the two of you? When Phoebe's not around?"

"He's a bit more relaxed. But...you see, the thing that bugs me the most is that he doesn't take control just in everyday life — but also in bed," he added quietly.

Francis' eyebrows shot up. "He's a top?"

Pierce nodded gloomily.

"That's a surprise. You haven't bottomed for a guy in ages, have you?"

"No, I haven't. Not before Noah. But that's not the point. I...like him topping, actually. He's good at it."

"But you want to nail his arse through the mattress once in a while too," Francis finished for him levelly.

"Yeah."

"Nothing wrong with that." Francis shrugged. "But he doesn't let you, I assume?"

"No. He doesn't...let me touch him that way and, generally, he's not much into cuddling anyway. He won't let me lead either."

Francis stared at the crowd of people unseeingly, thinking. "You know that some guys just don't like it or simply don't even want to try it, Pierce."

"But he has bottomed before and he liked it, he said."

"Did he tell you who with?"

"His first two boyfriends. Well, I suppose there's something else I should tell you." Pierce really didn't want to bring the matter up but he knew he had to, knowing it was the vital element to Noah's behaviour.

"What's that?"

"The first time I met him, he was...in training. With Robert." The thought still made him sick.

Francis' head jerked up. "He was with Robert? As a top?" A slow, wolfish grin appeared on his face. "Rob bottoming is something I never thought I'd hear of."

"No. Noah was his sub." Pierce squirmed at the twinge in his stomach.

Francis frowned. "Now you're confusing me. You said Noah's a top?"

"He is. I can't really explain why he did this whole submissive thing, France. He had his reasons. The thing is, I think Robert did some pretty twisted stuff with him. He fucked Noah and he wasn't exactly gentle with him. He also..." Pierce tried desperately to keep the bile from rising. "Robert offered Noah to me for a fuck and I... I took him. And hurt him. I knew he wasn't ready for it, but I did it anyway."

Francis looked at him steadily. "You fucked him although he wasn't ready?"

Pierce met his gaze, wincing. He knew it was unforgivable and was grateful that Francis refrained from telling him so. "Robert talked me into it. He claimed Noah liked it rough and he even got Noah to tell me that he could take it, although he so clearly wasn't ready. He still took it surprisingly well, but I know he must have been hurting throughout. I should have known. I just should have known. He said it wasn't the worst of what Robert made him do, either."

"Well, I suppose getting fucked by a handsome guy really isn't such a bad thing to experience in a building full of well-trained Doms," Francis said ironically. "But you think what Robert did with him left him traumatised, if I understand you correctly."

"Yes, probably, although I'm not sure. You're the expert in sexual hang-ups, but what I saw Robert do to him was nasty, to say the least."

"Have you talked to Noah about this?"

"No. I tried to, but he refuses to give me any more details or even talk about what exactly happened between them."

"How much do you know?"

"I didn't get many of the rules, but I think Noah wasn't allowed to make any sound. He certainly wasn't allowed to speak and when he...when he screamed because he was hurting, Robert said he was going to punish him for it. He used a whip on him, a bull-whip I think, and from the looks of it, he used it a lot. He had Noah collared and leashed, with nipple-clamps connected to his collar. It was like...his main goal was to hurt and humiliate Noah. At the time I thought Noah was your usual sub in training, you know, but he...he hated every bit of it. I noticed that he wasn't even hard when we fucked him, but I thought that maybe…uh, I don't know. I never would have done it if I'd known…" he broke off, feeling guilty and ashamed.

Francis had listened calmly, his face not showing any hint of what he was thinking. His voice was perfectly controlled when he answered. "Yeah, it sounds just like Robert's style. Taking a guy who's obviously a real alpha down a few pegs must be his idea of a wet dream."

"Noah isn't just dominant, he's also bloody proud," Pierce added. "He was majorly pissed off with me when I offered him a job, saying he didn't need me to support him."

Chuckling, Francis raised his eyebrows. "Seems you've got quite a handful with him." He became serious again and summed up Pierce's report. "So, Robert's training consisted of rules, education, of course, pain both mechanical as immediate and personal as educative punishment and definitely humiliation. And Noah's been solely responsible for a child since before he was twenty. What about his parents?"

"Booted him out 'cause he's gay just before Phoebe was born. They haven't spoken since. I suppose there's more to it, but that's all he would tell me."

Francis nodded thoughtfully. "Well. From what you told me I think your guy definitely is a perfect candidate for an issue or two, both sexual and psychological. I'm just not sure which ones exactly. I'd have to meet him, then I'll probably be able to tell you more."

Pierce smiled at him in relief. "I was hoping you'd say that. I arranged for him to meet us for drinks at five at Harry's Bar."

"You're being a bit presumptuous, aren't you?" Francis grinned.

"I just know I can rely on you."

"Save the flattery for your lover, Prince Charming. I've got the feeling he's gonna need it more than I do."

Pierce forced himself to finally ask the dreaded question. "Do you have a theory about him yet?"

Francis frowned. "Yes. But I'd rather keep that to myself until after I've met him."

"Okay. How's business going?"

"Fine. We're getting more applications for membership than we can accommodate. I'm actually thinking about expanding. Or maybe opening up a second club for a slightly different target group. Appeal to those who only come to play because they think leather's the latest fashion statement."

They chatted animatedly for another thirty minutes until it was time to go and meet Noah. Pierce was dreading it, but hoped that it might give him the answers he needed. Turning to his brother for advice and telling him all the intimate things about Noah had been a hard decision, but he was getting increasingly desperate to find a solution to what he knew was becoming a problem in their relationship. The sad truth was that, after four months, he had come to realise that he and Noah were not going to have a future if they didn't manage to balance their respective roles.

Noah was already at the bar waiting for them when they entered. Francis stopped dead when Pierce pointed him out. "That's Noah?"

"Yup." Pierce nodded proudly, mesmerised as always by Noah's exceptionally good looks.

"I need to talk to you right after this," Francis said urgently as they crossed the room to join Noah.

Pierce glanced at him. "Okay. Hello, darling." He greeted Noah with a soft kiss on the mouth. "This is my brother, Francis. France, this is Noah."

Noah and Francis shook hands. They ordered drinks and spent the next hour talking. Pierce remained mostly silent and listened. It was amazing to watch how easily Francis dominated the conversation and steered it in the direction he wanted, keeping Noah apparently totally oblivious that he was being interrogated. Francis asked Noah all kinds of questions about his life and Phoebe and, although his questions became increasingly private and delicate, Noah didn't seem to mind. He was unusually willing to confide in Francis on a certain level and didn't close up until Francis tried to make him talk about his parents — the ultimate touchy subject for him.

Eventually Noah glanced at his watch and startled. "Sorry, I really have to go. Phoebe's got to be in bed in an hour." He smiled apologetically and kissed Pierce. "Want me to come around later? Judith offered to stay with Pheebs."

Pierce nodded, delighted at the thought. "Of course."

"Okay. I've got some work to finish so I'll be there at around nine. Francis, it was nice to meet you. If I'd known Pierce has such a charming brother I'd have asked to be introduced earlier." He grinned, not quite flirting yet but definitely on his way.

"The feeling's entirely mutual, I can assure you," Francis said smoothly and smiled at Noah.

Pierce watched his brother's face curiously but in silence until Noah had left.

"So? What do you think?"

Francis let out a regretful sigh and met his eyes. "Sure you don't want to let him out to play? He's adorable. Shame you found him first."

"I'm absolutely sure. Go on, spill the beans."

Francis swirled the drink in his glass, staring at it thoughtfully for a while before he looked at Pierce. "Your pretty boy is pretty messed up. He's a complete control freak, you were right about that. The good news is, I think he's naturally inclined to be relatively moderate, a switch in all probability, so it's an acquired feature. He's so used to being in charge that he just doesn't really know when to back off, but I think he could learn that."

"What's the bad news?" Pierce enquired nervously.

"The bad news is that he's got serious trust issues. He has to be in control simply because he's never had anyone he could trust with it."

"Do you think that's why he keeps control in bed, too?"

Francis nodded. "Yeah. There's usually only two alternatives for guys like him sexually. Either they keep control over everything, including sex, which usually means that they're either singles, or if they have a relationship it is dangerously lopsided because they always dominate their partner. That's what Noah's doing, by the way."

Pierce pulled a face. "I thought so. What's the alternative?"

Francis grinned wickedly. "Some of the guys turn to the other extreme. They need someone they can trust and who helps them cope with their lives so much so that if they can't find that someone in their ordinary lives, they vent that need in a sexual context." He raised his eyebrows meaningfully.

"They turn to a Dom and submission," Pierce finished as the pieces clicked into place. "So what Robert did was essentially the right thing for Noah?"

Francis shook his head, looking annoyed. "What Robert did to Noah was unforgivable. First of all, Noah didn't come to him of his own free will, which is the first and most important condition to true submission. Second, you can't get a guy like Noah to submit by torturing him. It would break them eventually or leave them traumatised, but they'd never submit."

"What about Noah?"

"Noah is seriously traumatised. That's what I wanted to talk to you about earlier. I saw him before. At the club, with Robert. I just didn't make the connection straight away." The tone in Francis' voice sent a shiver of apprehension down Pierce's spine. "What happened?" he asked, dreading the answer.

"Robert had him in a public scene."

"Oh, fuck."

"Yes."

"Tell me," Pierce said quietly.

"He had him on the back stage, tied up and blindfolded. He whipped him and then…let a couple of guys fuck him in public."

"Bathroom," was all Pierce got out as he fled from the table. After several minutes of retching until nothing was left inside him, he was still trying to keep the images from appearing in his mind. Scenes like the one Francis had just described weren't unusual and by far not the most extreme thing that happened at the club. But unlike the men who usually participated in it, Noah wasn't into getting whipped, let alone being the bottom in a gang bang. Pierce felt his stomach heave again, but nothing would come out. He left the small cubicle and went to wash his mouth and face before he returned to Francis, who looked at him with concern.

"I'm sorry, Pierce," he said in a low voice. "But, if Noah agreed to it, there's nothing I can do about it."

"He didn't agree to it, though. Noah needed a lot of money because his daughter's seriously ill and Robert paid him to be his sub," Pierce forced the words out through clenched teeth.

"He paid him?" Francis's eyes went wide. "I'll need the details, but I can probably have him banned from the club for that if you want."

"Thanks. But it's Noah's decision. I'll try to ask him what he thinks."

"I'll probably boot Robert out anyway. He knows that it is against the rules."

Pierce chewed his lip gloomily. "What do you think I should do about Noah? I don't think either of the alternatives you mentioned is an option, to be honest. I don't think turning him into a sub is going to work, but I just can't keep putting up with him bossing me around either."

Francis shook his head. "No. It's not who you are. You're just too dominant yourself."

"So what do you suggest?"

Francis looked at him intently. "Right now, Noah's biggest fear is to lose control. The way I see it, there's only one way to make him overcome that fear."

"Which is?"

"He's got to face it. You've got to make him lose control entirely and, when he falls, you've got to be there to catch him so he knows he can trust you."

Pierce let out an uncertain chuckle. "And how am I supposed to do that?"

Francis shrugged. "Get him to submit."

"What? Didn't you just say that he's already traumatised because someone did that very thing with him?"

Francis met his anger calmly. "Yes. I'm not saying you should torture and humiliate him. There are different ways of making someone submit."

"But I'm not even a Dom, Francis. I don't know how to do this."

"I'd offer to take him on myself, little bro, but that wouldn't solve your problem. If you want to fix Noah and get him to trust you, that's the only chance you two have."

Pierce felt numb with fear, but if he could really help Noah with this… "What do I have to do?"

"Take it slowly. Be careful not to do anything that would scare or hurt him. After what Robert did to him, he's probably got quite a lot of triggers so the trick is to avoid them. Most importantly, no restraints, no sensory deprivation, no rules and no humiliation, but I guess you know that. Steer well clear of anything that might cause him pain, not even accidentally or just a little. Don't tease him either, he might misunderstand it. He needs to feel absolutely safe all the time. If at any moment he shows a sign of discomfort, don't just stop what you're doing. Back off, but don't let him fall. Keep physical contact with him. He'll probably respond well if you talk to him, but be careful what you say."

Pierce frowned. "So these are my rules, right? But what do they apply to? Where do I start?"

"Fuck him, of course," France said lightly.

"But he doesn't…"

"Pierce, Noah's a control freak. That runs so deep that he doesn't even let go in bed. You could start trying to take more control in everyday life, but I don't think it would work. In all probability, you'd just split up. I know that the mess Robert caused doesn't exactly make this any easier, but you could actually use it in your favour if you do it right. If you can get him to the point where he trusts you with taking control in bed, he'll let you take control in your everyday lives eventually too."

"What if I fail?"

"You'll lose him and he probably won't ever trust anyone again."

"I don't think I could stand that."

"Then don't fail," Francis said simply.

"When do I start?"

"Tonight."

"Tonight? But…"

"Tonight's as good as any night. I opened his mind to a few things today, Pierce. Trust me. Challenge him, take control. I assume you know what turns him on, so use his body to get his mind where you want it to be. You could put a cock ring on him if you think he'll let you, so he won't get distracted in case he can't keep it up again. Fuck him, make sure it's good for him and, when he gives it up to you, you can start pushing his boundaries. He probably won't do it tonight, but that's okay. Just don't push him too far. You know the signs when they submit, don't you?"

"Yeah, I guess I can tell. I just don't think I can get him there any time soon."

"Sometimes they get there faster than you think. Be ready when he does."

"Do you think I can do it?"

"You love him, that gives you an advantage. I'm a little worried about the details of his trauma and the triggers, to be honest, but as long as you don't experiment too much with him, you should be safe."

"Are you sure about this?" Pierce asked sceptically.

"Well, I suppose he could see a psychiatrist, but I don't think that would help him. Especially not if he doesn't think he's got trust issues in the first place."

"So instead you're sending me on a mission," Pierce groaned unhappily.

Francis smirked. "Yep. A sub-mission."

"Thank you, France."

"You're welcome. Good luck."

# Chapter Ten

Getting Noah into bed that night wasn't difficult. By the time he arrived at Pierce's home, he was already quite horny and a bit of naughty flirting worked its usual trick on him. Noah was obviously surprised when Pierce rolled on top of him soon after they had made it into bed, but didn't seem to mind.

Pierce felt his resolution quaver when he looked down into Noah's lust-darkened eyes. Those beautiful eyes had seen things he didn't even want to think about and now he was about to make Noah face his worst fear and strip him of his confidence. The thought made him feel like a traitor.

"What's up, baby?" Noah asked huskily, his hips pushing up to rub against Pierce's butt.

"Nothing." Pierce gave him what he hoped was a reassuring smile. "There's something I'd like to do, if you don't mind." He knew he'd have to get Noah very horny if he wanted his plan to work.

"What's that?" Noah's voice had dropped to that silky purr.

"Hmm, this." Lowering his head, Pierce very carefully sucked Noah's left nipple into his mouth. Generally, Noah didn't encourage Pierce to play with his body. Blowjobs were about the only thing Pierce was allowed to do to Noah.

"Pierce, what are you doing?" Noah sounded confused as Pierce started caressing the sensitive bit of flesh very gently with his lips and tongue. He ignored the question long enough to tease Noah's nipple into a tight little nub.

"What does it feel like?" Pierce asked softly, keeping his voice low and soothing.

"It... I don't know. You don't...oh." The little breathy sound Noah made when Pierce sucked on his right nipple was enough to tell Pierce that Noah liked this far more than he was letting on.

Pierce took his time caressing and nibbling, careful not to let Noah feel his teeth, all the time listening to Noah's breathing. After four months and a lot of sex, he could read the signs of Noah's body. When Noah's breath started coming in shallow gasps, he shifted his attention to other body parts, leaving a moist trail of kisses down Noah's flat stomach and further down to his thighs.

"Pierce, what...unghh, oh fuck, yes!"

Pierce effectively took Noah's mind off whatever he'd been about to say by smoothly taking him into his mouth and building up a nice firm suction, working Noah just the way he liked it. Soon Noah was panting and meeting Pierce's strokes with shallow thrusts of his hips. *Amazing how he can be flat on his back and get sucked off and still try to top*, Pierce thought and carefully reached out, holding Noah back with one hand across his waist.

Noah shifted under his grip, trying to find more friction, when Pierce slid his free hand down to play with Noah's balls. A needy little whimper escaped Noah's throat, but he didn't try to stop Pierce. Paying close attention to Noah's reactions, Pierce slid one finger behind Noah's balls, stroking the sensitive skin. As expected, Noah's body went rigid under his touch and Noah raised his head to look at him. He looked flushed and extremely turned on but at the same time highly uncomfortable. "What are you doing?" he asked quietly.

Pierce kept stroking Noah's stomach. "I'd just like to play with you a little. Touch you and kiss you, you know. Make you feel good."

"Yeah, but...don't... You know I don't..." Noah stammered, eyes wide with fear. He knows something's up, Pierce realised. "I'm not going to do anything you're not comfortable with, I promise. If you want me to stop, I will. But you get to do so much to me and spoil me rotten all the time. I'd like to give you some of that back." He wondered if maybe he should have crossed his fingers behind his back, but decided it hadn't been a lie. He did want to spoil Noah and make him feel good.

Looking up, he found Noah still staring at him, looking even more anxious.

"There's nothing to be scared of, baby. I just..."

"You want to fuck me, don't you?" Noah said abruptly.

"What? What makes you think...?"

"I knew you'd try it sooner or later. I was just hoping I had a little more time." Noah sighed.

"Noah, I'd never hurt you, you know that, right? I love you."

"And you want to fuck me."

There was no point denying it. Noah wouldn't believe him anyway. "Yes. Yes, I do. Would that really be so bad? I'll do anything to make it good for you. I know I can make it good for you."

Noah looked at him, a multitude of emotions flickering across his beautiful face. "Okay," he whispered, almost inaudibly.

Pierce was baffled. "Really?"

Noah nodded. "Yes. Do it. I'm sick of being scared."

This was not at all what Pierce had expected. "Are you sure?"

Noah sneered. "I told you that if I say something, I mean it." His expression turned softer. "Do it, Pierce. Fuck me." Closing his eyes, he turned his head to the side and spread his legs a little in silent invitation.

Pierce tried to swallow the lump in his throat and focused on Noah's body again. His erection hadn't survived their conversation, so Pierce decided to work on that first. To his relief, Noah's cock responded as usual. "Noah? Would you like me to put a cock ring on you?" Pierce asked softly, stroking him to keep him hard.

"Think that's gonna work?" Noah sounded sceptical.

"It should make it a bit easier for you. I'll use one with a snap button that will come off easily if you don't like it, okay?"

Noah nodded his agreement and silently watched Pierce carefully put the smooth piece of leather on his cock.

"How does it feel?"

Noah shifted a little and gave his cock a tentative tug. "Weird. Big. But I think it's okay for now." He didn't look convinced but seemed to accept it.

"Anything in particular you'd like me to do?" Pierce asked, a little uncertain. The turn of events had left him even more indecisive about how to do this. He had hoped he'd get away with just making it up as he went along, but it was getting more complicated than he'd expected.

Noah squinted at him. "Just do it. You know how it works."

Pierce grappled with the lube and slicked his fingers with a generous amount of it, inadvertently dripping some on Noah's stomach. "Sorry." He used the stray drops to slick up Noah's cock, treating it to a little extra attention. Noah groaned silently, seemingly enjoying it and Pierce gained confidence. As before, he slid his fingers behind Noah's balls, cautiously searching for the right spot. He moved his finger gently, trying to coax Noah's muscles into relaxation but they refused stubbornly. Noah shifted uneasily underneath him and Pierce wondered if trying to do this with Noah had really been such a good idea.

As soon as he pushed a tentative finger into Noah's body, he knew Noah wasn't ready for this at all and was having far more trouble with it than he was letting on. The muscles in his stomach stood out with tension.

"Shh, sweetheart, relax," Pierce cooed. "You're so tight, darling. I need to get you ready for me. Keep breathing." He carefully pushed in, only the fraction of an inch deeper, but it was too much.

"Get off me!" Noah suddenly screamed and jumped off the bed, knocking Pierce over in his haste to get away. He stopped in the middle of the room, shaking and covered in sweat, his chest heaving with rapid breaths. "Don't you ever touch me like that again," he snarled.

"Noah, I... I'm sorry," Pierce said, flabbergasted and trembling himself. "I thought you were okay, really, or I wouldn't have... I'm so sorry, really, baby. Shh, it's okay, I'm not going to hurt you," he tried to soothe, but Noah just stared at him in blind terror for a few moments.

At last he seemed to remember where he was. "Just don't... Just... Oh, forget it!" He started picking up his clothes and getting dressed with shaking hands.

"Noah, please calm down. It's okay, really. I'm not going to..." Pierce started, but Noah interrupted him harshly.

"No, it's not okay. Just don't ever try to do that again."

"I won't, Noah, I won't," Pierce assured. He took a few steps towards Noah and held out his hand, disappointed when Noah flinched away from his touch.

"Don't."

"But, Noah, can we please talk about..."

"There's nothing to talk about. I just need to be alone for a bit." Noah cut him off again, still battling for composure.

"What does that mean?"

"What I just said. I need to be alone." Noah had dressed in record time and shrugged on his jacket. "I'll call you."

"Will you really?" Pierce asked numbly, watching Noah open the door. Noah hesitated but didn't look at Pierce.

"Yes, but it might take some time," he said quietly and left.

Pierce was having more and more trouble concentrating on his work. Almost a week had passed since his attempt to gain Noah's trust had so seriously backfired. Noah still hadn't called and Pierce was beginning to wonder if he would at all. Noah did his job at Pierce's company as he was supposed to do, but carefully avoided meeting him. Every time Pierce tried to casually bump into him or track him down in one of the offices, Noah disappeared before he'd had a chance to talk to him. Pierce was just contemplating whether or not to ask his secretary if Noah was in the building when there was a knock on the door. Pierce's heartbeat sped up. Only two persons were allowed to do that without prior announcement from his secretary, she being one of them and she usually preferred to use the phone anyway.

"Come in," he called.

It was indeed Noah, who slowly opened the door and looked at him uncertainly. "Got a moment?"

"Sure." Pierce gave him an inviting smile and indicated for him to take a seat. "What's up?"

Noah remained standing. "I was just wondering... Do you want me to quit?"

"What?" Pierce asked, baffled. "Why would I want that?"

"Because...well, it seems it isn't working between us the way you want it to."

Pierce took a moment to digest this. "I'm very pleased with your work, Noah, I think you should know that and I'd hate to let you go. If you're unhappy about any of the contract details, I'm sure we can find a solution."

Taking in Noah's unusual shiftiness, he understood. It was what he had dreaded all along. "Is this really about work or are you..." He forced the words out. "Are you breaking up with me?"

"Pierce, I like being with you, I really do, but you're not going to get what you want from me and it wouldn't be fair on you to expect you to settle for that."

Pierce nodded slowly. "This is about last week, isn't it? Me wanting to fuck you." It wasn't really a question, but Noah nodded anyway, wordless.

"So you want to quit because I'm not getting what you think I want?" Pierce asked carefully.

"Well, it just wouldn't be fair, would it?" Noah answered, holding Pierce's eyes defiantly.

"Has it occurred to you that fucking you may not be the only thing I want from a relationship with you?" Pierce took a step closer to Noah, crowding him.

"What do you want then?"

Pierce didn't answer immediately. Instead, he left Noah standing in the middle of the room and went to the door. "Right now?" he asked and casually turned the key in the lock. "Right now I want you to bend me over that desk and fuck me for as long as you need to get that stupid idea out of your head."

He walked up to Noah, stopping so close to him he could feel his breath on his face. "And then I want you to stop making silly assumptions about what I want. Next time you want to know, just ask, okay?"

# Chapter Eleven

"So is there any chance we get to meet that new man of yours any time soon?" Pierce's mother asked nonchalantly in between tiny sips of her wine.

"My...what makes you think there is one?" Pierce knew that the silly grin on his face was giving him away. Besides, his mother was a very observant person. She had probably figured it out within about thirty seconds of seeing him.

"Well, the smile on your face is one thing. The fact that you've been trying to cancel dinner three times in a row is another. Would you mind telling us a little about him at least, since you obviously consider us unfit to meet him?"

"His name is Noah. Noah Conway. And you know I don't think you're unfit to meet him. It's just...well, things are still pretty fresh and, honestly, the prospect of meeting my parents seems to scare the poor thing quite a lot."

"He doesn't even know us and is already scared? Hm." She grinned playfully.

"I think he just can't imagine that you'd welcome him as the man who's taking your son to bed. You see, his parents weren't exactly sympathetic when they found out he likes boys."

"No? Well, if you keep referring to him as the man who's taking our son to bed, then maybe we won't be quite so sympathetic in future either," his father commented dryly. "What's he like?"

"Pretty gorgeous, Dad. One of the best-looking guys I've ever seen. He's also smart, funny, witty and has a six-year-old daughter." He watched two pairs of eyebrows raise simultaneously. "A daughter?"

"Uh-huh." Pierce drank some more wine. "He was with a girl when he was younger and, well, knocked her up."

"And how come the child's with him?"

After another rather large gulp of his delicious red wine, Pierce filled them in on the important details of Noah's life. Predictably, they were both aghast at the cruelty of Noah's parents turning him out and impressed by what Noah had achieved afterwards. By the end of the meal, Pierce knew they were both going to welcome him with open arms whenever he was ready to meet them, which was probably going to take some time yet. Even though they had officially established their relationship months ago, Noah still looked close to bolting whenever Pierce suggested they meet his parents for their monthly dinner together.

Pierce excused himself to go to the bathroom. Walking down the narrow staircase to the basement, he wondered once again why a restaurant that served such extraordinarily good food didn't make a bit more of an effort with its atmosphere. Not that the restaurant itself wasn't decorated tastefully and kept meticulously clean, but having to walk down a dank, narrow aisle past the storage rooms to get to the bathroom didn't exactly create a cosy ambience. He noticed that one of the doors to the storage rooms was standing ajar. Probably just someone filling up stocks. Well aware that he'd had too much to drink, Pierce went through to the bathroom, relieving himself and thinking about Noah and all the things he wanted to do to him the next time they met.

As usual, naughty thoughts involving Noah combined with the touch of his own hand got him painfully hard in an instant. Too bad his parents were upstairs, waiting for him to return in time for dessert. Sighing, he washed his hands and tried to think of unsexy things while he dried them. When his erection had faded enough for him to risk walking without damaging himself, he started his way back along the smelly aisle. The door to the storage rooms was even wider open and, when he passed it, he noticed that the lights inside were off. He hesitated briefly, wondering if it had just been left open accidentally and contemplating whether or not he should simply close it when he heard a muffled groan from behind the door.

He froze and listened intently. Another groan followed, longer this time, and then there were more sounds, something like a body shifting and a subdued whine. The only reasonable explanation Pierce could come up with was that whomever was in that room had probably stumbled in the dark and hurt themselves while getting supplies for the kitchen. It was the only reasonable explanation until he pushed the door open and took a step inside to help. His help was obviously not required by either the skinny figure draped over a stack of barrels in one corner or by the guy who stood behind him, pounding his arse with hard, fast thrusts. They seemed to be doing just fine and Pierce couldn't help grinning as he realised that what he had mistaken for the sounds of a person in pain were in fact noises of arousal—although, judging by how roughly the little twink on the barrels was getting fucked, he might very well be in some pain.

Pierce was just about to turn around and leave them to it when the taller guy tightened his grip on the boy's hips to pull the thin body closer and tilt his arse to the right angle, growling huskily when the movement deepened their contact. It was the exact same motion Noah often made in bed when he was getting close and wanted to get Pierce to finish, but it was the sound the man made that had Pierce stop dead and stare while his heart started hammering at a frantic pace. The height was right, as was the general shape, but it was impossible to tell since both men were still fully dressed apart from their trousers, which had pooled around their feet on the floor.

Bracing his hands on the barrel for leverage, the skinny guy pushed back harder and started babbling. "Yeah, fuck me, stud. Yes, oh yes, right there. Come on, Noah, give it to me!"

The floor started slipping from under Pierce's feet. No way. It couldn't be. The man currently buried balls-deep in some twink's body just couldn't be Noah. His Noah, the one who'd said he was meeting an important potential client and would turn in early when Pierce had suggested seeing him after dining with his parents. With amazing clarity, Pierce took in all the little details he hadn't noticed before. How the boy's legs were shaking with the effort of accommodating the taller man's strong thrusts, how sharply the man's fingers dug into the pale, bony hips to hold the slim body before him in place. The slapping of slippery skin against skin, the squelching sounds of the lube, harsh breathing and the occasional groans and grunts. The smell of male sweat and sex.

Pierce didn't need to wait any longer, didn't need to see the man's face. He knew the noises Noah made during sex well enough to realise that Noah was close and barely holding off. Even though he doubted that either of them would notice, he tried not to make a sound as he slipped out of the room, pulling the door closed behind him. Feeling numb, he climbed the stairs to finish dinner.

# Chapter Twelve

"What's up?" Noah asked softly. Standing behind Pierce, he pressed his warm, hard body firmly against Pierce's back. His arms closed around Pierce's waist, Noah rested his head on Pierce's shoulder, nuzzling the soft spot below his ear. "What's got you all tense, baby?"

He shifted a little, letting Pierce feel how turned on he already was. "Want me to relax you?"

Something inside Pierce finally snapped. He spun around to face Noah, pulling free with an angry sneer and enough vigour to send Noah stumbling back a few steps to regain balance. "Relax me? Is that what this is for you? A way to relax?"

Noah stared at him, eyes wide with surprise and confusion. "Huh?"

"Tell me, Noah—what does this mean to you?"

"What does what mean?"

"This." Pierce threw his arms up in helpless rage. "Us."

"What the fuck...?" Noah gaped at him blankly.

"What does it all mean to you?" Pierce repeated, wondering if he was making any sense.

"I really don't know what you're on about, Pierce."

"I just want to know what our relationship means to you. What do you think we're doing?"

"We're seeing each other, we're... What do you want to hear?"

"I want to hear what you think there is between us," Pierce explained, forcing himself not to shout.

"What do you expect me to say?" Noah's eyes narrowed guardedly. "You know what there is between us. We spend time together, we talk, we eat, we watch movies, we fuck—where does all that come from now?"

"That comes from the man who calls you his boyfriend," Pierce snarled. Running one hand through his hair, Noah looked at him, his expression somewhere between helpless confusion and anger. "What is this about, Pierce?" he asked exasperatedly.

"You. Me. Us. It's about where we stand as a couple and whether or not our relationship is working."

"Shit," Noah groaned. "I didn't even know we had relationship issues until now. What the fuck is wrong with you?"

"Friday night. The Taj Mahal. Your dick up that twink's arse in the basement."

Noah closed his eyes, swallowed and slowly opened them again. He took a breath to say something but changed his mind and started chewing his bottom lip instead. Pierce watched him, hoping against logic that what he had seen had somehow just been a dream, waiting for Noah to explain, to apologise, to say something, to just react.

At last Noah raised his eyes to look at him. "That had nothing to do with us."

"Nothing to do with us?" Pierce shouted. "It has fucking everything to do with us when you stick your dick in another guy's arse!"

"We never said we were exclusive," Noah said quietly.

"Fuck, Noah, what were you thinking? We're a couple, we agreed on that much, and you know how I feel about relationships. Did you really think it was okay to keep fucking other guys? And if you really did, why keep it a secret? If you honestly thought it was okay, you could have just told me instead of feeding me that crap about going to bed early because you had such a hard day."

Noah stared at him, defensive and subdued in the face of Pierce's rage, but remaining silent.

"Was he the first?" Pierce asked quietly. He didn't need to wait for Noah to say it—the answer was plain in his eyes.

"No, of course not," Pierce said hollowly and let out a grim laugh. "Silly me." He looked at Noah for a while, taking in the soft curve where his neck and jaw met, the clear, refined lines of the face he knew so well and the bright blue eyes he'd trusted, and suddenly he realised that he didn't know the man standing before him, had never even begun to really come close to him. The insight hurt more than the betrayal. "You've never even stopped seeing other guys, have you?" He barely recognised his own voice.

"What do you want me to say?"

"The truth would be nice for a change. Maybe you could start with what made you think fucking around was a good idea."

"I didn't think it was a good idea," Noah said evasively.

"Obviously that didn't stop you from doing it."

"No. No, it didn't." He took a deep breath. "I'm not sure why I did it. I guess it was just easy. Being with you...it's all so complicated, so intense. I know you don't like bottoming. I just wanted to... I want to fuck someone who actually appreciates it once in a while."

Pierce stared at him, shell-shocked. "You fuck dumb little twinks because you think I don't *like* it?"

"Well, you don't," Noah pointed out.

Pierce took a step closer, forcing Noah to back away, and glared at him. "Don't you dare make this about me," he snarled. "And just so you know, you're wrong there. I like it, which doesn't mean that I wouldn't like to give you a good hard pounding too—but that's your real problem, Noah, isn't it? You know that I'd fuck you as soon as you'd let me and that's what you can't handle. I know that what happened with Robert has left its scars on you but I'm sick of being the one who has to pay for it. I've tried everything I could to make you feel safe, to prove to you that you can trust me, and all I get in return is you keeping your distance and turning to boys who don't care about you and are happy to just take what you're giving. I told you that I want us to be partners in this, Noah, but it doesn't work if you don't let me in and take what I can give you every now and then too." Catching the flicker in Noah's eyes, he added, "I don't mean sexually. I've accepted that that's a no-go for you and I wouldn't dream of pushing you after what happened the last time. But you don't even let me into your life, Noah. You just do your thing and I get to tag along whenever it suits your plans."

"I told you, Pierce. You knew my priorities before we started this and you wanted it anyway. I told you I couldn't promise you anything."

"I know your priorities, Noah. But this isn't about that either. Phoebe is fine, she likes me, I know that and I adore her. We get along well, and she's totally okay with us. Seeing you happy makes her happy too, don't you understand that? Why can't you just accept that instead of trying to keep us all apart? Why can't you just let us be the family we could be instead of destroying it all just so you don't have to let me come close?"

Noah had remained completely silent throughout Pierce's outburst but finally he snapped. "Because I just can't, okay?" he hollered. "I can't. Phoebe is... She's all I have and... It's not going to work. I can't let you take that away from me. If I let you in and... I can't let that happen. I just couldn't take that, Pierce," he broke off with a choked sound.

"I know," Pierce said softly, finally understanding Noah's truth. "I'm sorry, Noah. I really thought we could make it work."

"Well, it has worked for the past months, hasn't it?" Noah said hollowly.

"Yes, somehow it has—in a very crooked, distorted way," Pierce admitted. "Only because I kept thinking you could change, though, but I've finally realised that you're never going to and I can't go on trying to have a relationship with someone who so obviously doesn't need me. If you ever do, you can give me a call."

"You know that's not going to happen," Noah replied quietly.

Pierce took a deep breath and nodded. Time to let go. "I know. Tell Phoebe I love her and wish her all the best, especially for the operation. Take care." He didn't turn around, didn't look back, didn't even look up until he had left Noah's flat and reached his car. He got inside and started it, driving mechanically and somehow hanging on until he was in the safe haven of his home, where he could finally allow himself to go to pieces.

# Chapter Thirteen

"Noah?" Pierce asked in a low voice.

"What is it?" Noah's head jerked up from the plastic cup he was toying with restlessly.

"Nothing." Pierce smiled. The drained expression on Noah's face slowly changed to one of recognition. "Pierce?" He blinked a few times. "You're here?"

"I'm here," Pierce stated, forcing himself to sound calm.

"Gosh, for a moment I thought I was hallucinating," Noah sighed tiredly.

"No, I'm real, I promise."

"I know. A hallucination couldn't possibly look so gorgeous," Noah said and instantly lowered his head, looking a little embarrassed. He had clearly said more than he'd intended to.

Ignoring the slip, Pierce gave him a gentle smile. "How's Phoebe?"

"She's doing surprisingly well given the circumstances. She seems more fascinated by the funny way the doctors speak than by what they're doing with her. She's still asleep and the nurse just booted me out. Said I should go for a walk and she'd page me when Pheebs is awake and they start getting her ready for surgery." He snorted irritably and held up a small black plastic item. "As if. But apparently that's their routine." He looked up at Pierce with red-rimmed, tormented eyes. "How can something like that ever be routine?"

"I suppose it is for them." Pierce shrugged and carefully sat down on the hard plastic chair next to Noah's. "How are you?"

"Okay," Noah answered promptly.

"Let's try again, shall we? How are you?" Pierce repeated.

Noah smiled sheepishly. "Holding on."

"Barely, from the looks of it," Pierce commented dryly. "When was the last time you slept?"

"Last night."

"Slept properly, in a decent bed, not dozed off from exhaustion in a hospital chair."

"Oh, that. Uh, not sure. Must have been at some point last week."

"More like last month the way you look, but I'll let it pass for now," Pierce said sternly. "Food?"

"Not much point—can't keep it down anyway."

Pierce groaned. Noah seemed to be living on caffeine, judging by the rather impressive collection of empty plastic cups next to him.

"That's what I thought. You know, I saw a rather inviting-looking cafeteria on the way in. Care to give it a try?" Pierce offered.

Noah glanced at him briefly then shook his head. "No thanks. I'd rather wait here in case she wakes up."

"I thought so." Pierce smiled and pushed a brown paper bag into Noah's hands.

"What's that?" Noah took the bag gingerly, frowning.

"Sandwiches. I didn't know what you'd be able to get down, so I brought something for your sweet tooth as well. Chocolate muffins," he explained with a grin.

"Thanks, but there was no need to..."

"Yes, there was," Pierce interrupted him sternly and pushed the bag into his hands. "Take your pick but eat at least two items. You're no help for Phoebe if you've starved yourself to death by the time she's ready to go home."

"I'm not..." Noah started, looking slightly annoyed at being ordered around, but obediently opened the bag, selected a sandwich and took a reluctant bite.

"Good boy," Pierce said softly then turned serious. "Sorry I cut it so late, by the way. I would've been here earlier but first my flight was cancelled and then the plane got delayed. I meant to arrive last night."

"How come you're here anyway?" Noah asked in between swallowing and taking the next bite.

"I promised," Pierce said simply. "I said I wouldn't leave you to deal with this on your own, didn't I?"

"Oh." Noah was spared a more elaborate answer when a door opened and a nurse appeared.

She was blonde, pretty and the smile on her face was a little wider than the professionally comforting one her job required. "Noah? Phoebe's awake now, you can see her. I figured you were still here, so I didn't bother paging you." Seeing Pierce next to Noah, she added, "I see you found some company. How nice." She turned to Pierce. "Are you related to one of our patients?"

"No," Noah quickly said. "He's...uh...he's..."

"A friend of the family, actually," Pierce filled in smoothly, smiling at the adorable blush on Noah's face.

"Oh, I see. You're from England too, aren't you?"

"Yes."

"It's really kind of you to come all the way over here to support Noah and Phoebe. I'm sure they appreciate it a lot."

"I do," Noah said softly. "Would you like to say hello to Phoebe?"

"Of course, if that's okay. I'd love to."

Noah cast the nurse an anxious glance but she smiled apologetically. "We're already getting her ready for surgery, Noah. I'm afraid there's barely enough time for you to see her." She looked at him thoughtfully then sighed. "But since I need to verify your contact details I don't think anyone would mind if he snuck in quickly just to wish her good luck."

"But my contact details..."

"Need to be verified just once more," she cut him off determinedly and waved for him to follow her with a conspiratorial smile. Pierce didn't miss the way she looked at Noah when he walked past her into the nurse's room. Someone had got himself an admirer. Smiling, he went into Phoebe's room. He barely had time to enjoy the delighted smile she greeted him with and exchange more than a few words with her before the nurse was back with Noah and ushered him out.

Noah followed a few minutes later, looking more terrified than ever. Pierce took a few steps and carefully put an arm around his shoulders. "She'll be okay, Noah. Everything will be fine, you'll see."

Noah nodded but didn't meet his eyes. "I hope you're right. I really do."

For the next five hours, Pierce did his best to take Noah's mind off what was going on behind the big grey double doors to the surgery. They watched surgeons and nurses come and go and, every time the doors were opened from the inside, Noah's head jerked up and his face turned pale with fear, but no one ever said anything other than 'We're still working on her, Mr Conway. We'll let you know if anything happens'.

Whatever conversation Pierce started, Noah wasn't paying attention. After a while, Pierce gave up trying to get him to talk and just watched him battle his demons in silence.

"Noah," Pierce said after what seemed like an eternity had passed. "Sit down for a minute, will you?"

"I can't," Noah replied unhappily.

"If you keep pacing like that, you'll end up being charged for a new floor," Pierce pointed out.

"If I don't, I'll explode."

"No you won't. Sit down. Have a drink, I got you some juice."

"I can't."

"Yes you can. Stop being a drama queen, it doesn't suit you," Pierce said sternly and held a bottle of apple juice out to Noah. Noah looked at him unhappily but took the bottle. Pierce wordlessly indicated the chair next to his own, relieved when Noah sat down at last. "She'll be okay, you'll see," he said for what must be the hundredth time.

It had become a mantra, something Noah seemed to need to hear every couple of minutes. He never gave an answer to it and Pierce had given up expecting one hours ago. It was hard to bear, but there was nothing else he could do for Noah, who struggled to hold on so bravely.

"What?" Noah asked a little self-consciously, having noticed Pierce's lingering glance. Pierce smiled.

"I was just thinking that you're by far the most amazing guy in this building." He kept his voice low enough so the nurse scuttling past couldn't hear. "I'm proud of you, you know. You're holding on really well."

"There's not much I can do right now, is there?" Noah's voice had that hollow tone it assumed when he was struggling with his emotions.

"I know. You're here. You made sure she's given the best chance she could get."

Noah sighed. "I just wish it was over already."

"It's at least another two hours," Pierce reminded softly.

"I know." Noah stared blankly at the big, grey double doors again. "Thank you," he suddenly said.

"What for?"

"Being here. I know I'm not exactly great company right now but... I appreciate it. A lot. I don't know what I'd do without you here."

Pierce shrugged. "You'd get by, just like you always do."

"She's missing you, you know," Noah started cautiously. "Keeps asking if you're coming to see us again."

Meeting Noah's eyes, Pierce didn't miss the unspoken question. "I'm only here to see you through this, Noah," he said gently.

"Oh." Noah fidgeted with the juice bottle, picking at its label with unsteady fingers for a moment before he quietly answered, "I thought maybe...uh, I don't know, maybe we could..."

Pierce shook his head regretfully. "This doesn't change anything between us."

Noah nodded sadly, took a breath and exhaled slowly. "I see."

Pierce hesitated for a moment, then sighed and took Noah's hand in his, giving it a reassuring squeeze. Neither of them said anything else as they continued waiting in silence.

When the scheduled time was up, still no one showed and the minutes seemed to pass even more slowly than before. Noah had started pacing again, unable to keep his nerves under control any longer when at last a surgeon approached them.

"Mr Conway?" He looked at Noah with an unreadable expression on his tired face.

"Yes?" Noah spun around, staring at him with wide, terrified eyes and his whole body started trembling. Pierce put an arm around his shoulders in support, ready to hold him upright if he had to. His own heart jolted painfully with dread for Phoebe.

"Phoebe is fine and stable. Everything went according to plan."

Noah let out a strangled sound somewhere between a sob and a sigh. "She...she is really okay?"

"Yes. She's still asleep though, and will take some more time to wake up."

"Why?"

"That's nothing to worry about, Mr Conway. She's strong and she will hurt less when she's asleep."

"Can I see her?"

"Yes, of course. She probably can't hear you, but you can talk to her anyway if you want."

Noah took a step but stopped and turned back to Pierce. "She made it," he whispered hoarsely.

"I know," Pierce smiled. "Go on, see her. Tell her I love her."

"Aren't you coming?"

"Do you want me to?"

"Of course I do. So would she." Noah grabbed him by the hand and completely ignored the surgeon who took a breath to say something but just sighed instead and let them pass.

Pierce was shocked at the sight of Phoebe's tiny, fragile body attached to lots of quietly beeping machines by thin tubes that protruded from various parts of her body. He heard Noah inhale sharply at his side. "She's okay, love," he said softly, giving Noah's trembling hand a squeeze. Watching Noah look at Phoebe, telling her in a low, tear-choked voice how much he loved her and that she was going to be okay, was heartbreaking to witness. After a few short minutes, the nurse came in and wordlessly beckoned Pierce out. He cast a brief glance at Noah, who was completely oblivious to anything around him, then followed her out.

"I think it's best if Noah gets a few minutes with her in private," the nurse said apologetically and showed Pierce to a waiting area. "I'll let him know you're waiting there," she added.

"No need to. I'm leaving," Pierce said curtly.

"But you only arrived yesterday," she pointed out, surprised.

"I know. I came to help Noah get through the surgery, that's all."

She looked at him thoughtfully. "A friend of the family, huh?"

Pierce gave a non-committal nod.

"I suppose I'm wasting my time if I keep asking Noah out, am I right?" she asked calmly.

Pierce smiled at her. "I suppose you are."

"Too bad." She sighed. "Well, I guess it's true what they say. The best ones are either taken or gay. Or both. Well, in that case, all the best for the two of you. Or rather the three of you." She turned to go, but hesitated and looked at him again. "I know it's none of my business, but if I were you, I wouldn't leave him alone for so long in a situation like this. He really needs your support."

Pierce looked at her in surprise. "I think you're misunderstanding something here. We're not a couple."

"You're not? But I thought..."

"Look, I've no idea if he's seeing someone, but the other assumption applies, I'm afraid. But then again, maybe not. He's not the exclusive type and it's hard to tell where he wants to put it next, so maybe you should just try your luck anyway. As far as I'm concerned, you're welcome to have him."

Her eyebrows shot up. "Whoa, easy, tiger. Your feelings are hard enough to knock people unconscious. What happened?"

"It's a long story, and frankly, it is none of your business. I'm only here because of Phoebe."

She nodded slowly. "I see. But even though it's none of my business I hope you know that he's going through hell without you."

"You think so?"

"It's obvious. Before you turned up, he was barely hanging on. It's remarkable how he keeps it up while Phoebe's around, but as soon as she's not, he's close to cracking up. Whatever happened between the two of you, I hope you'll sort it out."

"I don't think we will."

"Too bad. The way he looks at you, like you're the world to him—I wish someone would look at me like that one day."

"I guess you're wrong there. His world consists of Phoebe and himself, and he's not willing to change that."

She sighed dismissively. "I think you're wrong there, but apparently you're just as stubborn as he's reclusive, so suit yourself." With another pointed sigh she rolled her eyes, turned around and left him alone.

# Chapter Fourteen

"Pierce?" The voice was slurred, barely audible over the background noise of a full pub and huskier than usual, but it was unmistakably Noah's soft, melodic drawl.

"Do you have any idea what time it is?" Pierce snapped sleepily.

"One? Ish?"

"Quarter past. Are you pissed?"

Noah let out a low chuckle. "I guesh I might be a little drunk," he admitted cheerfully.

"Is Phoebe with you?"

"Coursh not. She'sh with Judish. Judith." He was obviously struggling to remain comprehensible.

"What do you want?" Pierce asked, none too friendly. There was a long silence on the other end. All Pierce could hear was Noah's uneven breathing and he wondered if Noah had simply fallen asleep. When the answer came at last, there was a loud roar in the background and Pierce wasn't sure he'd heard him correctly. "What's wrong with you?" he asked with increasing concern.

"I know I shaid I wouldn't call, but I...losht control. I'm a little drunk and...I need you now," Noah drawled. 'A little' was clearly an understatement.

"Where are you?"

"Here."

"Ha ha, funny," Pierce grumbled. "Where the fuck are you?"

"Harry'sh Bar."

"I'll be there in ten minutes. Don't go away, don't do anything stupid. Have some water, but for God's sake don't have another drink, okay?" Not waiting for the reply, he switched the phone off, slammed it on the table and grabbed his clothes. It took him nine minutes to get to the bar and another five to find Noah in the crowd. He was slouched on a bar stool at the back of the room, looking like he was about to pass out. Seeing the glass of water Noah was nursing obediently, Pierce couldn't help smiling. "Drink up, I'm taking you home," he said by way of greeting.

"Thatsh the besht offer I've had all night." Noah grinned goofily.

"Hopefully the only one you've accepted, too," Pierce muttered under his breath as he slung Noah's arm across his shoulders and dragged him the exit. "Fuck, you're heavy," he grumbled on the way to Noah's car. Noah was evidently barely able to walk and Pierce forced himself to concentrate on steering him clear of street lamps and similar obstacles rather than allowing himself to dwell on memories of the first time they had left the bar together.

"I mished you," Noah cooed.

"I'm sure you did," Pierce replied vaguely. "Now can you stand upright for as long as it takes me to open the door? Where's your key?"

"Search me." The sudden naughty grin on Noah's face was unmistakable.

"You wish. Where's the bloody key?" Pierce repeated in an undignified tone, watching the playful expression fade from Noah's eyes as quickly as it had appeared.

"Shomewhere… Uh, in here, I think." Noah fumbled in his pockets with a shaking hand.

Amused in spite of himself, Pierce watched him for a few moments before giving in. He slid his hand into the inside pocket of Noah's jacket, trying to ignore the alluring scent of leather mingled with Noah's warm body. His fingers met metal and he was half relieved, half disappointed at his instant success as he pulled Noah's key ring out. He quickly unlocked the door, keeping an eye on Noah who still looked like he was about to drop to the floor, then carefully helped him into the car. By the time he had made it to the driver's side, Noah had already passed out. Pierce watched him for a few moments, taking in the lines on the face he used to know so well. There were a few that hadn't been there before and he couldn't remember the hollow cheeks and dark shadows under Noah's eyes, either. Sighing, he started the car and drove the short distance to Noah's home. When he cut the engine, Noah opened his eyes sleepily and gave him a lopsided smile.

"Let's get you inside so you can sleep it off," Pierce whispered and helped him out of the car and into the house.

"Take off your jacket and sit down. I'll get you some more water." When he returned with the glass, Noah was staring at him with a strange expression in his eyes.

"What?" he asked uncomfortably.

"I mean it." Noah held his gaze even though it visibly took him some effort to keep his eyes from crossing.

"What? Here, drink this so we can get you into bed."

The naughty expression instantly returned to Noah's eyes. "Why don't we forget about the drink and go straight to bed?"

With a sigh Pierce mentally cursed himself for having come to Noah's rescue. Taking Noah to bed was extremely tempting, but not an option. He did have principles, after all, so all he was going to do was tuck Noah in and leave him to sleep it off.

"Drink," he insisted and pushed the glass into Noah's hand.

"Think you'll manage to clean your teeth? I'll take this through to your bedroom." He led the way through Noah's small flat, relieved when Noah followed him and obediently went to the bathroom, careening rather precariously around the corner.

Somehow Noah seemed to manage performing his bathroom routine. When he entered the bedroom, however, it became obvious that he intended to perform even more.

"Noah, where are your clothes?" Pierce groaned.

Noah smiled sweetly. "Don't need them. C'mere." He looked a lot more sober than before.

"Cut it out and just get into bed, will you?" Pierce snapped. Really, Noah drunk, naked and visibly horny was more than he could handle.

"Only if you join me."

"You know that's out of the question."

"Why?"

"Do I really need to tell you?" Pierce snarled irritably.

"Please don't carry grudges, baby," Noah crooned. "I'll make it up to you."

Pierce laughed hollowly. "Really? And how would you do that?"

"I'll let you fuck me."

"Fuck, Noah, exactly how much did you have to drink?"

"I'm serious, baby." Noah's voice was low and seductive. "You know you want to and I certainly want you to."

It took Pierce a few seconds to find his own voice. "It used to be the last thing you wanted," he said at last.

Noah took a few steps, which brought him within inches of Pierce. "I've changed my mind. Come on, Pierce. I want you. I want it. Fuck me. Make me feel it."

He was close enough for Pierce to feel the heat of his body and the scent of him brought back memories of all those nights they had spent together. Suddenly, Pierce could no longer deny the effect Noah had on him and arousal kicked him firmly in the groin. So close... He didn't know who made the move to cover the last few inches and it didn't really matter anyway. His lips met Noah's, relishing the firm softness. When Noah's tongue found his, he couldn't help but answer its beckoning.

# Chapter Fifteen

"Mr Hollister? Mr Conway is here to see you, sir. Can he come in?"

Pierce groaned and hesitated for a moment before he pushed the talk button.

"Did he say what he wants?"

"No, sir." His secretary sounded surprised. "Should I ask him?"

"No, it's okay. I'll see him." Whatever it was, it was nothing she should be bothered with. Pierce made a mental note to officially cancel Noah's special status. Not so long ago Pierce's secretary had been under order to rearrange entire schedules if Noah wanted to see him. At least she was alert enough to realise that he was no longer to be admitted instantly.

Noah himself was apparently just as alert. The door was opened almost reluctantly and the expression on his face as he entered was wary and unusually shy.

"Hello, Pierce. Thanks for seeing me."

Pierce chose his most business-like voice to answer. "No problem. What can I do for you?"

Noah met his eyes but quickly looked away again. "Nothing, I suppose. Although I was hoping... Uh, never mind," he interrupted himself.

"Why are you here?" Pierce asked, not bothering to hide the impatience in his voice.

Noah squared his shoulders. "I'm here to apologise," he said flatly.

"What for?"

"Making a complete dick of myself and putting you in an awkward situation. I'm sorry."

"Oh." Pierce took a moment to look at Noah. Sober, Noah looked more like his usual self but still quite worn out and weary.

"Apology accepted. I just hope Phoebe didn't have to see you like that. How is she?"

"Fine. She's recovered perfectly, even better than they expected, and no, she didn't," Noah said defiantly. "She spent the night with Judith, otherwise I would have never let it get that far. You really should know me better than that."

"That's great news, really," Pierce said, sincerely relieved. "I'm happy for the two of you. You must have had a hell of a hangover, though. You were completely wasted," he couldn't help needling.

Noah sighed. "I know. I didn't really mean to let it get that far, or maybe I did, I don't know. Anyway, I got there pretty fast."

"How much did you have?"

"Not sure," Noah shrugged. "You know I rarely drink, so when I do it doesn't take much to take its toll on me."

"Yeah, I remember." He remembered, indeed. The few occasions when Noah had actually allowed himself to drink more than half a glass of wine for company had invariably left him with fits of giggles and extremely horny. Fortunately, with Noah alcohol never killed the ability as it increased the willingness. Repeatedly, Pierce had had to force himself not to try to get him drunk just to enjoy an almost all-night romp. He tried not to remember too much and focused on the far less pleasant present instead.

"Well, anyway…thanks for taking me home," Noah said.

"You're welcome," Pierce answered and fell silent. There wasn't really anything to add. Noah had said what he wanted to say, they had made the appropriate amount of small talk, so now they had no excuses left to delay Noah's departure. Judging by the expression on Noah's face, he had come to the same conclusion. "Well, I guess I'll just leave you to your work then," he said quietly and turned to leave.

"Take care," Pierce replied numbly, surprised by how much it still hurt to watch Noah go. Noah lingered at the door. "I miss you, you know," he whispered.

"I miss you too, but I'm afraid that doesn't change anything."

"I know. I just thought…maybe you'd like to know. Anyway, thank you."

Pierce frowned, confused. "You already said that."

"No. Thank you," Noah repeated with a different intonation.

"What for?"

"Not accepting my…offer."

"What off—Oh. Er, it's okay. So you remember that?"

"Yeah, I remember." Noah sounded more than a little embarrassed.

"How much do you remember, exactly?" Pierce asked.

"The details are still a bit fuzzy. I remember kissing and there definitely was some mutual stroking involved but that's about it. I know you didn't fuck me, though, I'd remember that. Besides, even if I didn't, I'd probably still be feeling you."

"I knew you didn't mean it," Pierce stated.

At last Noah turned around and looked at Pierce. "I did mean it. I wanted you. I wanted to feel you...inside me."

"But you don't bottom. Ever. You made that perfectly clear."

Noah sighed. "I know. I used to enjoy it, you know. That night, with you... I wanted you to have me that way. I knew you could make it good."

It took Pierce a moment before he trusted his voice enough to answer. "Noah, you were pissed. You wanted a fuck and knew I wouldn't do it so you came up with what you probably thought would tempt me the most and, admittedly, I was tempted. You almost got me, but we've been through this before. Even though we both prefer to top, sex was never really the problem for us. You're a great lay, but a couple of good fucks just isn't what I want from you. For a while I thought we wanted the same things, but you made it perfectly clear that we don't. What you can give me is just not enough. I need more than that."

Noah stared at him for a long moment, a silent struggle in his eyes. "I know," he choked out. "But the thing is, I have nothing left to give. I'm sorry," he said quietly and turned to open the door but hesitated. "I did mean it, you know," he added in a hoarse whisper.

"Mean what?"

"That I need you."

"You do?"

"Yes." Noah nodded unhappily. "Phoebe's operation…you there. I don't know how I would have got through that."

"I don't think I did much to help," Pierce said uncertainly.

"But you did, Pierce," Noah protested earnestly. "You kept telling me that everything would be okay. I was mad with fear of losing her, you know. I was just so fucking scared and I… You saying it would be okay kept me sane. I never realised how much I need you until that moment."

"Oh, Noah," Pierce groaned. "I'm glad I could be there for you and Phoebe, but you know it doesn't work between us. We don't work."

"I know. I know, and I'm sorry I messed up. I keep wondering what would've happened if I hadn't…cheated on you."

Pierce winced. "It probably wouldn't have changed much. We'd have split up eventually anyway. You fucking around was just the catalyst."

"You really think so?"

"Yes," Pierce confirmed steadily.

"You're probably right. I'm sorry. Take care." This time, Noah had the door open and slipped through it without further hesitation.

# Chapter Sixteen

"Noah finally broke," Francis announced brightly.

"Hu — what?" Pierce suppressed a curse as he watched his coffee spill out of the broken cup to find its way along the floor.

"Noah. Remember him? Pretty guy, sexy as sin, more issues than the Playboy. You used to go out with him."

"I remember Noah," Pierce snapped.

"Good. I thought so."

"I especially remember breaking up with him."

When it seemed Francis didn't intend to comment on that, Pierce sighed and cautiously asked, "What do you mean, 'he broke'?"

"Ah, so you were listening." Francis laughed quietly. "Why don't you come to the club and find out?"

"He... Noah's at your club?"

"Yeah."

"What happened?"

"I'll tell you when you get here," Francis said slyly and hung up.

Pierce stared at the beeping phone for a while before he pushed the off button irritably and went to fetch his coat.

It took him less than two minutes to track his brother down inside the club. Francis had settled into his preferred private space at the back of the club, twisting a glass in his fingers and apparently lost in thoughts. A second, untouched glass stood on the other side of the table. Pierce sat down, ignoring the drink, and glared at Francis indignantly. "Mind telling me what's going on now?"

Francis looked up, an exhausted but definitely smug expression on his face. "Hello bro. Glad you could come."

"Cut out the foreplay, France. Tell me. What did you mean with 'Noah finally broke'? And what makes you think I'm even interested to hear about it?"

"Well, he did. Gave it up to me completely. Gosh, that guy is something. No wonder you're mad about him. He's adorable."

"Francis!" Pierce said sharply. "I'm not mad about him. I'm not even seeing him any more." Francis shot him a knowing, indulgent glance and smiled softly. "You're not going to tell me he's playing in your club, with you, are you?"

"Well, I wouldn't exactly call it playing." Francis held up a hand. "All right, all right, don't bite my head off. I'll tell you. I'm just still a little shaken up, so take it easy on me, will you?" He took a sip from his own drink before he continued. "Noah's been coming to see me for a while now. He wanted to work on those issues of his and, well, tonight we had the big breakthrough at last."

Suddenly changing his mind about the drink, Pierce downed half of it in one gulp. He put the glass down, picked it up again and drained it before meeting Francis' eyes. "Tell. Me. Everything. Right from the start," he ordered and picked up the bottle to pour himself another drink. Francis' eyebrows shot up and he took the bottle from Pierce's hands. "You don't want another drink. Danny's going to bring you some water."

"I fucking well do want another drink," Pierce grumbled and reached for the bottle again.

"No, you don't. Trust me," Francis said in that voice he used to check undisciplined subs. Nice and friendly with only a hint of a threat that disobedience wouldn't go unpunished. Pierce pulled his hand back.

"Why not?"

"Because I want you to be sober for this conversation and especially when you see Noah."

"I'm not going to…"

"As I said," Francis cut him off and dropped his voice to a conversational tone when Pierce fell silent. "He's been coming here for quite some time. He realised he's got serious issues and he wanted to get over them." He smiled affectionately. "He's been working incredibly hard."

"Fine. So you've got a new pet who makes you happy. What does it have to do with me? We split up almost half a year ago, in case you don't remember."

Francis grinned. "He's not my pet. Unfortunately. He knows exactly who he belongs to and so do I, by the way. Now, why do you think he came here?"

"How would I know? Maybe he took a liking to the scene after all."

"No, he didn't. He merely understood that it was a way to help him deal with all the crap he's been through."

"Oh, really? Are you fucking kidding me? Part of his problem was getting tortured into submission by a sadistic Dom, so how the hell does getting himself whipped some more help him overcome his trust issues? Or the fact that he's a stuck-up control freak?"

"He didn't get himself whipped. Not that I wouldn't be very happy to put some marks on that flawless skin of his, but unfortunately that's just not what he needs. There are ways of making someone hand over control other than causing pain."

"Please don't tell me you fucked him," Pierce groaned.

Francis chuckled softly. "We agreed that I didn't need his sexual submission to take him where he needs to go. A pity really." He sighed regretfully. "That body…" He met Pierce's eyes across the table and winked. "Don't worry, I didn't so much as touch that pretty cock of his, just got an eyeful every now and then. As I said, we both know who he belongs to." He grinned mischievously. "You let him top, didn't you? Ah, you're a very lucky man."

"If you didn't whip him and didn't have sex with him — what did you do with him?" Pierce asked with a frown.

Francis gave him a soft smile. "First I merely got him to be still and think a lot. He was so tense and jumpy he'd bolt as soon as I touched him, so I helped him build up a basic trust level until I got him to the point where he'd lie down and let me give him a massage — in an entirely non-sexual way, I assure you. Eventually he trusted me enough to let me tie him up for the massages. That was when I started getting him to talk. He's been astonishingly open about his emotions ever since I got him to trust me with his body." He met Pierce's eyes. "He's been through a serious lot of shit. It's his crap, so I'm not in the position to tell you, but I suppose he will tell you anything you want to know."

"You tied him up for massages?" Pierce raised his eyebrows in disbelief. "He wouldn't even let me touch him unless it was to bring him off. Don't tell me you've flogged him, too."

"No, I haven't. Although I've used it to stroke him. He doesn't need pain but it helps him concentrate if he can't move, so I put him in bondage several times," Francis explained calmly. "Besides, he loves getting touched and cuddled—he's just never learned to appreciate it."

"I still can't believe you're using your Dom techniques on him." Pierce was beginning to long for that drink again.

"Why not? It's not all just about pain and kinks, you know. In fact, most of it is about trust and support, caring for someone and helping them tackle and work through their issues."

"I keep forgetting about that degree in psychology you hold," Pierce sighed.

"Will you keep it down? Like I'd want people here finding out about that," Francis muttered in alarm.

Smiling reluctantly, Pierce remembered how thrilled their parents had been at Francis' university degree in psychology. They hadn't been quite as thrilled when he'd started using what he'd learned to build his reputation as one of the best Doms and eventually open his own club instead of a practice, but they had long since accepted his choices.

"Does Noah know?"

"No. He came to see me to ask how you were and we started talking. I explained a few things to him and he decided to give it a shot rather than try a more conservative therapy."

"That's still quite remarkable considering what happened with Robert. You'd have thought he'd stay clear of anything remotely connected to the scene." Pierce pointed out, causing Francis to grin.

"How do you think they met? It's not that Noah is totally kink-free, he's just scared of admitting it."

"Hang on. What kinks are we talking about here?"

Francis' grin widened. "That would be for you to find out. We didn't go there, but, lately, being tied up gets him hard and my guess is that he'd take toys quite well."

"Toys?" Pierce asked blankly. "He won't even bottom and you think he'd like having a toy stuck into him?"

Francis' smile turned compassionate. "He doesn't want to bottom because it makes him feel out of control, not because he doesn't like it. In fact, I think he's going to enjoy it a lot."

"Yeah, just that he doesn't do it," Pierce snorted.

"Oh, he will, I'm sure of that."

"You shouldn't hold your breath."

"I wouldn't. Breathing through it is best in my experience."

"Funny." Pierce glared at him irritably and took a sip of his water. "That's all very well, but I still don't see where that concerns me."

"He did it for you," Francis said simply.

"For me? I never asked him to come here and, well, do whatever he did."

"I know you didn't. That's what makes his gift to you all the more valuable. He's completely devastated about having fucked up your relationship and apparently some of the things you told him when you broke up with him hit home, so he's been trying to sort himself out for months to get you back."

"He...no way. Not Noah. He wouldn't. He's a mess, that's obvious, but according to him, everything's just fine. I've decided to take his word for it." Pierce's voice sounded bitter, even to his own ears. "I can't be with someone who doesn't need me and doesn't even want to be in a relationship. Losing him hurt too much, Francis. I can't go through that again."

Francis looked at him levelly. "Do you know his father beat him into hospital when he found out he was gay?"

"What? No, he just said it didn't go down well with them and that they weren't supportive of him and Phoebe. He never said..."

Francis let out a humourless snort. "'Not supportive'? They kicked him out and said they were going to have him arrested if he so much as tried to call them. He hasn't spoken to or heard of them since." He looked at Pierce intently for a moment. "He was eighteen, Pierce, he was just a kid. Do you really think he could just move on? Do you think it's easy for him to have a relationship with a man when that's the very reason his own parents detest him?"

"Well, he doesn't seem to have a problem having a physical relationship with a man. Or maybe I should say several of them."

Francis sighed irritably. "I know he cheated on you and I'm not saying that's okay. What happened back then almost destroyed him. It could have made him deny his sexuality altogether but it was certainly enough to make him feel uncomfortable about it. Sex is one thing—a relationship is something entirely different. He's only ever had random sexual encounters. Getting off with a guy just isn't the same as living with him, so the closer you got, the more he had to come to terms with and accept that he's gay. That's part of what made him freak out and run away."

"He didn't run away. He lied to me. He fucked other guys."

"He didn't at first. It wasn't until you tried topping him that he did it."

"Now where's the comfort in that?" Pierce huffed indignantly. "Besides, if I remember correctly, you were the one who told me I should do it. Make him face his fear, as you called it."

"I know, I know," Francis said unhappily. "The idea behind it was basically right but unfortunately his trauma wasn't quite what I thought it was. Giving up control is just a part of it—accepting who he is is even harder. See, that's why I told you back then I should take him on myself."

"Well, you did now, didn't you?"

"I did in a way, but I'm not what he ultimately needs. I can make him think and talk, put him through therapy, but I can't give him the love and acceptance he craves."

"And you think I can give him that? That's bollocks, France. It's too late. He made it very clear that he doesn't need me in his life and that I'm not what he wants." Pierce swallowed around the tightness in his throat.

"Well, as I said, he's realised that he was wrong. And he has proven that there's a lot he was not only willing to change, but has changed." Francis leaned in closer, his voice dropped to a soft, comforting whisper. "He's deeply in love with you, Pierce. That man would do anything to get you back. He's been through a lot and he both needs and wants you." He sighed. "Seriously, Pie, some of the crap I dragged out of him was just horrifying. There was more than one time when I wasn't sure if I could stand to go through with it, let alone make him face it. But your brave boy just kept fighting until we had each and every one of those old wounds ripped open, dissected and bandaged. I'm not saying he's completely healed yet, but he'll get to where he can handle the scars."

"What about my wounds?" Pierce asked quietly. "He already hurt me once. I don't think I can trust him with my heart again."

"Well, of course, I can't give you any guarantees, but he loves you. He really does. He's been proving it for months." His eyes softened even more. "See him. Talk to him. You'll understand. He's faced and fought his demons—now it's time for you to face yours. He deserves another chance. And so do you. I know you still love him, so don't throw this away."

"Fine. I'll see him. But only because you, dear brother, are by far the worst demon I've ever had to face. Where is he?"

"The white room."

"Is he…?"

"All nice and cosy, tucked up in bed. He might be asleep—he was pretty exhausted when I left him."

"Fine. I'll go and see him."

"Good boy. Take it easy on him, though. He's emotionally raw at the moment and has basically no defences left so I need to make sure he doesn't lose it entirely when he sees you. Tag along, I'll take you." Francis got up and led the way.

# Chapter Seventeen

"Noah?" Francis asked quietly into the dimly lit room, giving Pierce a signal to stay behind and out of sight. "You okay, sweetheart?"

"Yes, sir." The answer came in a quiet but steady voice.

"Did you rest a bit?" Francis went inside and crossed the room to sit at Noah's side on the huge bed. Pierce slipped noiselessly into the room, but soon realised he needn't have bothered. Noah's full attention was directed at Francis.

"Yes, sir."

"How do you feel?"

Noah hesitated before giving the answer. "Good, sir. A little...fragile, but calm." He took a breath. "Safe."

"You know what happened, don't you?" Francis softly stroked his hair.

"I think I do, sir."

"How does that make you feel?"

Again, Noah took a moment to consider his answer. "Good. Proud." He smiled softly. "Relieved, sir."

"You did exceptionally well today, Noah."

"Thank you, sir."

"Remember I promised you a reward?"

"I think I've already got the best reward I can hope to get, sir."

"Explain." Francis continued touching Noah, running his hand along Noah's bare arm in long, soothing strokes.

"Well, sir, quite simply feeling this way. Knowing what I've achieved. It's…rather enthralling."

"It's amazing," Francis stated calmly. "And I want you to know that I am very, very proud of you. Sit up now, please, Noah, and look at me." He waited patiently for Noah to disentangle himself from the sheets and obey before he slipped one hand around the back of Noah's head, cradling it and pulling Noah closer. "You really did very well. You've been to the edge, you've jumped and you've come out all the better for it. You still have some work to do, but this was the ultimate step."

"I know, sir. Thank you," Noah answered quietly.

"We'll keep the sessions going for some time, though, until you're a bit more settled, and remember, I'll always be here for you, understood?"

"Understood, sir."

"Very good, sweetheart. This is as far as I can take you, so that leaves us with the matter of your reward." He quickly glanced at Pierce, unnoticed by Noah, who was still entirely focused on Francis. "I know you said you already had the best reward you can hope to get but you should know that I like to exceed expectations. Anyway, this is your reward for your impressive battle."

Pierce left his hiding place next to the closet and slowly walked into the middle of the room. Noah's eyes widened as he recognised Pierce and a huge smile lit up his face. "Pierce!" His arms twitched in what was obviously the urge to throw the blankets off and jump out of bed to fling himself at Pierce, but he checked himself and looked up at Pierce with surprise, confusion and hope all written across his face.

"Hello, Noah," Pierce said softly. "You look…good. A lot better." Noah did indeed look better, albeit exhausted and tired, but the dark shadows under his eyes were gone and he seemed to have put on some weight. His upper body had regained its former muscle tone quite nicely, as Pierce could see.

"Thank you," Noah replied quietly.

Francis stared at them both for a moment, then bent over Noah, kissed his forehead and got up, leaving his place at Noah's side. "I'll let you two catch up now. Take all the time you want. If either of you needs me, I'll be downstairs. Don't hesitate to call me."

Pierce blocked his way. "Sir?" he asked with raised eyebrows.

Francis smirked and shrugged airily. "Well, I am a Dom, aren't I?" He brushed past Pierce and left the room, closing the door with a silent click.

Pierce turned to Noah who met his gaze, eyes a little wider than usual but outwardly calm. "Are you okay?"

"I think I am now." Noah smiled tentatively. "It's good to see you. I've…missed you. A lot."

"I don't really know what to say," Pierce admitted into the silence that settled between them.

"I know," Noah agreed. "I feel the same. I… I thought a lot about what it would be like to see you again and what I'd say to you, but right now it seems my mind's gone totally blank. Wanna sit?" He shifted a little, making more room so Pierce could sit on the side of the bed without having to touch him.

"Thanks." Pierce sat then grinned, indicating the blanket. "You are at least partly dressed under there, right?"

Noah returned the grin. "Nope. Part of your brother's session, but I promise I'm not going to fling myself at you. Not unless you ask me to, that is."

"I don't think that's gonna happen, Noah," Pierce said earnestly.

"No, probably not." Noah's smile faltered and he sighed regretfully. "Look, I know I fucked up. I'm sorry. Really. Deeply sorry. I'm not going to say that I don't know why I did it, because I do know. I know it now. Francis has helped me figure it all out, which doesn't really make it any better, of course. I just...uh, I'm not sure if it would help at all, but...if there's anything you want me to tell you, I will."

"You could tell me why you cheated on me," Pierce said with a calm he didn't feel.

Noah took a breath and squared his shoulders. "I was scared, Pierce. I was scared shitless, although I didn't realise it at the time. But the way it was between us... You got too close for me and I didn't know how to handle it. I've spent all those years being the only one I could count on and I couldn't just allow you to be there for me. I was too scared to trust you so I tried to keep you at bay. That's why the closer you got, the more you tried to prove to me that you cared and that I could rely on you, the more I had to push you away. And then that night when you...almost fucked me, I just freaked."

"Because you didn't trust me not to hurt you," Pierce prompted bitterly.

Noah frowned, big blue eyes sad but earnest. "No. Because I realised that I did. I knew you wouldn't hurt me and, even worse, I wanted it to happen. I wanted to feel you in me and I wanted to give you all of me. Ironically, that's what scared me to death." He swallowed tensely. "You were right, though. It was a lot easier to just do it with guys who didn't care about me because then I didn't have to worry about what it means to give myself away."

"Noah, bottoming for a guy doesn't mean you're giving yourself away."

"It does for me," Noah whispered. "It's not so easy to explain—somehow it's all tied to what happened when my parents found out that I'm gay."

"You never told me what happened, although, from what Francis said, I gather it was pretty tough for you."

Noah looked at him miserably. "Do you really want to know?"

Pierce shrugged. "Francis dragged me here tonight because he wanted me to talk to you. I'm here now, so we might as well talk."

"Okay. How detailed do you want the answer to be?"

"There's nowhere I have to be right now, you know. I want all the details you're happy to give, Noah, but you don't have to tell me anything that makes you uncomfortable."

"No, it's okay. I promised I'd tell you." Noah took a deep breath and let it out in an unhappy sigh.

"Tell me," Pierce urged softly.

Noah glanced at Pierce gloomily in the dim light. "I'd never realised there was something unusual about the fact that I liked looking at boys, you know. Where I grew up, that was just something you weren't supposed to do and no one ever spoke of it, so I didn't either. I hadn't even known that something such as being gay existed—it was simply unthinkable—so I would look at girls with the other boys, talk about girls with them, and think that one day I'd find a girl I liked and...we would do the stuff the older guys always talked about. You know, kissing was about as far as my imagination would stretch at that point. I'd kissed two or three girls by then, but I didn't really know how to take it any further.

"Then one afternoon, after school, I hung out with one of the older guys. He was the older brother of a classmate, quite popular and handsome as fuck. A real looker, and of course I was so impressed by the fact that someone like him wanted to spend time with me that I didn't think much about any of the others being around. I didn't think much about him taking me to an old shed where they stacked hay, either. Once we were there, though, he..." Noah broke off with a sigh.

"Please don't tell me he assaulted you?" Apprehension rose inside Pierce.

Noah smiled sadly. "No. No, he didn't. At least not in the original sense. He kissed me. He was really gentle and I'm sure he would have stopped if...if I had asked him to."

"But you didn't?"

"No, I didn't. There was something about him...being so strong, so tall, so...hard and just being him—it just blew my mind. It was the first time I got off on nothing but snogging and I was confused and scared as hell. It was a revelation, really."

"And you had sex with him?" Pierce prompted. Noah smiled faintly and shook his head. "Nope. I just came in my trousers. He was really careful with me and gave me all the time he thought I needed. We'd sneak out to meet in secret and just talk and kiss most of the time. After about two months he gave me my first blowjob. He taught me how to return the favour soon after that, but it took almost four months until he fucked me for the first time."

"Not what you expected?"

Noah pulled a face. "I hadn't really known what to expect and it was...pretty weird, you know? When you grow up not only thinking you're straight but not even knowing that there's an alternative, you just don't expect to find yourself in a haystack one day with another guy's dick up your arse."

"You bottomed." It wasn't a question.

"Yeah, I did," Noah confirmed, aware of Pierce's insinuation.

"Did you like it?"

"Mostly it hurt. I guess he hadn't done that part too often himself, so he just didn't know how to prepare a guy, plus we didn't have proper lube. I couldn't walk straight for about two days, but it was okay. Being with him in that way was worth it."

"Did you love him?"

"No. I liked him, but we were never in love."

"How old were you?"

"Sixteen."

Pierce tried to imagine Noah at age sixteen. He'd been nineteen when the photograph with Phoebe had been taken. So young and almost still a child himself. "What happened?"

"We spent a couple of months playing around then he had to leave for university. I was pretty disappointed but eventually I met someone else."

"Phoebe's mother?"

Noah shook his head. "Another guy. The way it went with him was almost the same, although we started fucking much sooner. We still met in secret, but it had been going on for so long that we became pretty reckless about where we went and if someone saw us together. We didn't even really think we were doing anything wrong, you know. We just knew we had something that was different to the others and we didn't want to run around rubbing it into their faces. So, one night, he walked me home and kissed me goodnight and my father caught us. We'd thought he had already gone to bed, but he'd waited up for me and seen everything."

"How did he react?" Pierce pressed softly when Noah was reluctant to continue.

"I'd never seen him like that. He was shouting and swearing at me." Noah's voice dropped so low Pierce could barely hear it anymore. "He…he beat me up until I thought he'd kill me. Well, actually, until I wished he'd just kill me. I don't know how long it took until he stopped. He probably only stopped because his own arm hurt too much to hit me anymore. Then he took me to my room, made me sit on a chair and tied me to it. He said I was the worst piece of shit he'd ever come across and that he damned the day I was born, but that he was still going to give me time to think about what I had done and get back on the right path."

"Oh God, Noah, that's…disgusting. I'm so sorry, baby." Pierce started stroking his shoulder in an automatic, comforting gesture. "How could he do that to you?"

Noah let out a strangled, bitter chuckle. "My family are strict Catholics. I guess he was convinced that I'd end up burning in Hell and it was his duty to save me from it. He took that duty very seriously. He kept me locked up for a couple of days. I only got a bit of water and food every now and then and he'd let me use the bathroom once in a while but he'd beat me with a cane or his belt twice a day. He didn't let me wash and I was covered in blood and hurting like hell. I was terrified he'd ruptured something inside me but he just wouldn't back off until I started pissing blood. He still kept me in until the worst cuts and bruises had faded but at last he took me to see a doctor. My kidneys had been damaged from the beatings, so the guy put me on antibiotics and sent me back home."

"He sent you back home? Didn't he see what had happened?" Pierce asked, horrified. He couldn't hold back any longer. Uncertain how Noah would react, he leaned in and wrapped his arm around Noah, surprised when Noah actually snuggled into the embrace.

"He had been very careful about his choice of doctor. The one he took me to shared his opinion on a lot of things and when my father explained to him what was wrong with me, and that he was doing it all just so I would understand how very wrong my behaviour had been, of course the guy agreed with him. He even suggested putting me on medication to stop those unnatural urges, as he called it, but my father didn't take him up on that, probably because it was too expensive. Eventually he let me out to go to school, but he kept a very close eye on me. When I so much as cast a glance at a guy, he got his belt out and gave me a piece of his mind."

"What about your mother? Didn't she have anything to say about this?"

"My mother? No. She thought he was right. She was just embarrassed that one of her children had turned out so rotten and hoped that my father would get the reins back on me. Eventually I didn't try to fight anymore. I'd learned my lessons and I knew what I was supposed to say and do. The beatings stopped simply because I didn't give him a reason for it anymore, but he remained suspicious 'cause I was never spotted with a girl. By that time I was old enough to leave for university, but he wouldn't let me because he didn't want to let me out of his reach in case I took advantage of my freedom. I really wanted to go, so I gave them what they wanted.

"I found a reasonably pretty girl, asked her out a couple of times and made sure half the town got to see me kiss and fumble with her. I think we went too far on that, in fact, since we got told off for indecent exposure in public by the police one night. My parents weren't too happy about that either, since technically I was supposed not to have any kind of intimate relationship before marriage, but I guess they were just happy I'd been caught with my tongue down a girl's throat and my hands up a skirt that time."

"So if you were not supposed to have sex before marriage, why did you do it with her anyway? You could have just waited until you were out from under your parents' hold. You didn't marry her, did you?" Pierce added.

"We didn't get married. But the thing is, I was eighteen, I'd been used to getting laid on a pretty regular basis and I was horny as hell. She was cute and although she didn't really turn me on, I was young and easy enough to manage to go through the routine." He let out a short, bitter sneer. "She wasn't too happy that I preferred doing her from behind and refused to go down on her, but I made sure she got her share of fun out of it, too. I kept her satisfied enough to make her stay with me and my parents seemed to buy it. They even agreed to let me go to university.

"Then, about a week before I was due to leave for university, David—my first lover—came back to visit his parents. He didn't know what had happened since he'd left and was eager to pick up where we'd left off. So was I and we fucked ten times in two nights and one afternoon. When I got back to my parents' place after spending the second night with him, she was there. She'd just found out. We'd only been together for about four months and I must have got her pregnant rather early on. Of course my parents twigged instantly what was cooking. I got home at eight o'clock on a weekday's morning and had just been fucked until I could barely stand upright and my alleged girlfriend sat at their kitchen table, crying her eyes out because she was pregnant with my child."

"Not a nice scene," Pierce managed to get out through the tightness in his throat. "What happened then? Your father, did he…?"

"No. I'd already told him that the next time he hit me I'd hit him back and he had an injured arm that day anyway. I'm not sure what would have happened if he'd tried it, to be honest. Their first solution was that we should get married, of course, but, fortunately, she refused. She freaked completely when I told her where I'd been and said she wasn't going to have the baby. In the end, I talked her into keeping her and giving birth and promised I'd take care of the child and she'd never have to see her again. My father kicked me out that very day."

"And you've really never spoken to your parents since?"

"No. As far as I'm concerned, their existence ended when I left their home. I wouldn't want Phoebe to meet them anyway."

"Sorry, sweetheart." Pierce continued tangling his fingers through Noah's hair, something Noah seemed to like a lot. "No one should have to go through something like that."

"Don't be. It's not your fault."

"I know it's not. But it's not yours, either."

"I know. It's what Francis keeps telling me. It's what I've been telling myself for years but I couldn't help thinking what it would have been like if I wasn't gay, if I could have been the son they wanted."

"Is that why you didn't want to be with me? Because you think it's essentially wrong to be gay?"

Noah smiled softly. "You see, that's the point. I don't think it's wrong. Not as such. I just think...well, my life would probably have turned out easier if I preferred pussy over cock."

"Noah!" Pierce yelped in mock alarm. "You kiss your daughter with that mouth?"

Noah grinned. "Aw, come on. That's what it all comes down to, isn't it?"

Pierce smirked and nodded. "I'm just glad you didn't decide to force yourself to rearrange your preferences."

"Oh no, I couldn't." Noah shuddered. "I found that out for sure when I faked it with Phoebe's egg donor. You know what it's like when you're young. Some days even a lamp post looks fucking hot. I suppose that was the only reason I could do it with her at all. After David returned and we fucked, I knew for certain that girls would never do it for me. Couldn't even get it up watching porn anymore unless the guys in it were really hot. And even then I'd usually fantasise about them doing me rather than being the one who gets to do the girl."

"Really?"

"Oh yeah. Boy, the first time I watched gay porn I didn't know where to look. Took me about three seconds to come."

"Well, that's pretty interesting, but what I meant was your fantasy was to be the one who gets fucked?" Very slowly, a wicked grin spread across Noah's face as he understood. "It's been a while, Pierce, but I remember liking it a lot when David fucked me. In fact, I rarely ever topped him at all 'cause I just liked it better when he fucked me right into next week."

"So how come you didn't like it after that? Was it all just because of...Robert?"

Noah still flinched at the name but he gathered himself quickly. "He was the first who hurt me," he said in a low voice. "The reason I didn't want to do it with any of the guys I picked up at random is simply that, for me, it's just too...intimate. I tend to get pretty emotional and that's not something I could let happen with any of them."

"Oh, Noah, always the control freak."

"Well, it's better to be a control freak then getting emotionally attached because you got a good fuck, isn't it?"

"Depends," Pierce said thoughtfully.

"On what?"

"The guy who fucks you."

"I know. That's what I'm saying. It's something I can't just give to anyone."

"You said you wanted to do it with me, though."

"I know. I did." Noah took a breath and exhaled slowly. "I still do. I'd love to be with you that way. Feel you in me, on me, taking everything I have to give..." Trailing off, he looked at Pierce miserably. "But I guess I blew my chance, didn't I?" he asked in a small voice.

"I'm not sure, Noah. You hurt me. A lot. I just don't know if I can trust you enough to let you in again. I'm not sure if I can believe that I'm not going to get hurt again. Francis said you're trying to change, but I just don't know if that's enough."

"I know. I know, Pierce, and I can't give you any guarantees. I just…hoped that maybe if I figured out what exactly my issues are I could fight them so at least they wouldn't get in the way anymore. I know I'll still be me and I'll never be able to shed the past completely, but I also know that I want to be with you. I love you, Pierce. You're the best thing that's ever happened to me apart from Phoebe and I don't want to accept that I've thrown it all away just because…just because I didn't even realise how stupid I was." He sighed. "But it's really up to you, I guess."

Pierce looked at him for a long moment. "There are a few things I want you to be clear about, Noah. First, I don't think you were or are stupid. I think you've been through a lot and it's probably affected you in more ways than I can imagine. Second, you can't shed your past and I wouldn't want you to be anyone but you anyway. Third, I guess Francis was right about you. You've come a long way and you deserve another chance for that. I still love you, Noah. I'm not sure if that's enough to make it last, but it's enough right now to keep me from accepting that it's over." He watched the smile spread slowly on Noah's face, watched the blue eyes brighten with exhilaration as his words were beginning to sink in.

"Are you really completely naked under there?" he asked idly.

"Uh-huh." Noah nodded softly.

"Hm." Pierce bent down slowly, holding Noah's gaze until he was too close to focus and their lips met with a shy, tentative touch. Noah's tongue slid out, coyly licking at Pierce's lips, asking to caress and affirm rather than play. Sighing, Pierce opened up and let him in, loving the way Noah's familiar taste filled his mouth and the touch of the supple wet tongue.

Eventually Noah retreated, keeping just enough contact to lure Pierce into his own mouth as he sank back onto the pillow and pulled Pierce on top of him. The kiss deepened and Pierce's hunger to taste and feel grew with every gentle lick, every sensuous swirl of tongues. A low, breathy moan came to his ear and he couldn't even tell who made it. Another, more urgent moan came definitely from Noah who pushed up against him, holding him tightly while moving in a gentle, unhurried rhythm.

"I want you," Noah breathed into their kiss. "Please. Fuck me. Let me feel you."

"Oh God, Noah," Pierce groaned, fighting for control. Noah begging to be fucked. A dream come true.

"Sure?" he forced himself to ask.

"I've never been surer of anything in my life," Noah panted, sliding his hand to Pierce's crotch. "Fuck me," he repeated breathlessly.

"How...?" Pierce looked down at him uncertainly.

"Just like this. I want to be able to see you." Noah spread his legs and pushed his hips up again.

"I just hope neither of us is going to regret this," Pierce sighed and gave in.

It took them less than thirty seconds of combined effort to get Pierce out of his clothes and under the thin sheet. They both moaned at the first contact of bare skin and didn't seem to know where to put their hands first. There was just too much to touch, too much to make up and Pierce didn't really know what to do.

Noah's body was still so familiar but his reactions had changed. He no longer took the lead and tried to get down to business instantly the way he used to do. Instead, he held back and let Pierce explore his body, openly appreciating each and every one of Pierce's touches. After a while Pierce dared himself to find out how much Noah had really changed. Sliding his hand between Noah's legs, he played with his balls for a bit before he moved further and found the tight little spot with his fingers. Noah tensed instantly at the contact and Pierce had an unwelcome flashback of the last time they'd tried this. Again, Noah was concentrating too much on what was happening when he needed to feel, not think.

"Roll on your stomach, baby," Pierce said in a soft voice.

Noah glanced at him with wide eyes.

"No need to worry, love. I'm not gonna fuck you from behind. I just need you to relax a bit, okay?"

Noah looked sceptical but turned on his stomach. Pierce gently nudged Noah's legs apart and settled between them, cupping Noah's tight buttocks with his palms. Lowering his head, he licked a long, moist line from Noah's shoulder blade to his left butt cheek. Noah shuddered delicately. Pierce repeated the action on the other side then drew tiny circles at the small of Noah's back with the tip of his tongue.

Noah's breath hitched when Pierce's tongue slid further down for a more intimate touch. Pierce took his time to caress the sensitive skin with butterfly licks, listening to the breathy whimpers Noah made before he dipped the tip of his tongue into Noah's body.

"Fuck, Pierce! What...yes, oh yes...feels...so good..." The whimpers turned into breathless gasps and Noah pushed back, welcoming the slick intrusion without thinking.

Pierce pulled him up on his knees for better access and started slowly fucking him with his tongue, keeping the touch gentle and shallow while stroking Noah's rock-hard cock with one hand at a measured pace.

Tremors ran through Noah's body as he rocked between Pierce's hand and tongue. He wasn't so much trying to take control as merely reacting on instinct in a helpless, unconscious rhythm, captured by the intense double stimulation. Pierce waited patiently until Noah arched his back, ready for more, before he carefully inserted one finger into Noah's body, still flicking his tongue over the soft skin. When he gently pushed in, Noah sucked in his breath with a low hiss.

"You okay?" Pierce whispered, relieved when Noah looked up at him and nodded.

"Just not used to it anymore."

Noah's words turned into a soft moan when Pierce pushed deeper, searching for the sensitive little spot inside with his fingertip.

He knew he had found it when Noah groaned and pushed back against him. Pierce replaced his tongue with another finger and took his time massaging the tight ring of muscles into relaxation. He hadn't known how Noah would react but it had definitely been the right move. Apparently Noah had never been on the receiving end of a rim job but it had worked magic on him. Noah's muscles were relaxed and supple, and, judging by the sounds he was making, he was well beyond any coherent thought. And fear.

"Turn on your back, love," Pierce instructed softly, giving Noah space to move.

Not daring to risk doing anything that would make Noah uncomfortable, Pierce removed his hand for as long as it took to apply a generous amount of lube then carefully sought out the little opening again.

When he pushed in with a third finger, Noah barely seemed to notice and Pierce continued caressing him, still watching every reaction of Noah's body closely. Every time Pierce's fingertips brushed his gland, Noah shuddered delicately and made a sweet little whimpering sound.

Keeping Noah spread with three fingers now, Pierce slicked his cock with his other hand and angled himself. A smooth replacement would probably be easiest for Noah. The grip of Noah's warm, velvety insides around him as he pushed in was almost too much for Pierce. Although he had prepared Noah well, he was still tight, but then he was bound to be. It had been almost a year.

Pierce refused to think about the first time he'd fucked Noah. As far as he was concerned, *this* was the first time. The first time it was just them anyway. No Robert, no pressure, no condom. Just their bodies, joined. He looked down to meet Noah's eyes and held them as he started moving slowly, carefully assessing how much Noah was able to take.

When he was sure that Noah was ready and willing for more, he thrust harder and deeper, loving the way Noah's body opened up for him. Their eyes remained locked throughout. The blue of Noah's eyes was dark with arousal but the frightened expression in them had been replaced by something that looked a lot like trust.

Noah had obviously really worked through his fear and was ready to let Pierce take charge. Watching Noah completely lose himself, Pierce's rhythm faltered as he finally recognised the signs. Noah was stunningly beautiful in his submission. Trusting and open, he allowed Pierce to take all of him, and at last, Pierce understood what submission was really about. He bent down for a loving kiss, just as Noah's head jerked back and a full body shiver rocked him.

For the first time in their relationship, Noah screamed with pleasure as he came. His muscles rippled around Pierce's cock, gripping him so tightly he lost control and followed Noah into sweet oblivion. Sweating and panting, Pierce held Noah in his arms for a long time, simply listening to their breathing and Noah's excited, beating heart slowing down to normal. He knew his world had changed.

"I love you, baby," he whispered into Noah's sticky neck.

"Love you too," Noah answered, nuzzling Pierce's ear.

"Do you really?" Pierce still didn't quite dare believe him.

Noah nodded. "'Course I do."

"But you never said anything. Before today, I mean."

"I always thought you knew."

"How could I when you never said it?"

"But... Oh, well, I guess I see your point." Noah smiled sheepishly. "I don't exactly show you much affection, do I?"

Pierce looked down at him earnestly. "Nope. I think the most affection you showed me was calling me baby and sticking your dick up my arse."

"Oh. Really?" Noah looked genuinely concerned. "I guess I suck as a boyfriend, don't I?"

Pierce nodded, smirking. "Yes, you do, and that's only ever good if it involves a blowjob." He turned serious. "The thing is, you're actually very affectionate. You can't seem to go an hour with Phoebe without telling her that you love her and how adorable she is. You just don't do it with me."

Noah frowned. "Are you jealous of Phoebe? She's my child, you can't compare that."

Pierce sighed. "I know you adore her and that she'll always come first. It's just nice to know that you care about me, too. I don't want to feel like a convenience for you to get your rocks off."

Noah's eyes widened in surprise. "Is that how you felt with me? I never saw you that way, though."

"There were times when I was pretty certain that was all I was for you."

"No!" Noah protested. "You're a lot more than that and you have been pretty much right from the start. I really thought you knew that."

"That just wasn't enough for you," Pierce said bitterly.

"You're still mad at me for cheating, aren't you? If it's any consolation, the guys I fucked in between were just a convenience. I told you why I did it. It had nothing to do with you."

Pierce sighed. "I guess I understand why you did it and I'm not mad at you anymore."

"No?"

"No. But actually, since you brought it up, I keep wondering if you would do it again." He held up his hand. "Think about it."

Noah shook his head. "Don't need to. If you're asking if given the same situation I'd do it again, then, yes, I probably would. I needed it at the time. I couldn't handle what we had. But if you want to know if I'd do it again now, then the answer is no, I wouldn't. I'd be yours exclusively for as long as you'd have me. I know how much I hurt you and I couldn't live with myself if I did that to you again."

Pierce held his eyes for a long moment before finally answering. "It hurt a lot, that's true. However, it wasn't the main reason I couldn't be with you anymore."

"What was?" Noah frowned.

"The fact that I never knew what I meant for you. You were always so fucking proud and independent and obviously doing fine without me. It's not nice being with someone who doesn't need you."

Noah reached out to cup the back of Pierce's head and gently pulled him closer until their noses almost touched. "But I do. I need you. I need you in my life and, if you want me to show you more affection, I promise to tell you that I love you at least once a day." He swallowed uneasily. "You know, my biggest worry used to be what I'd do if I lost Phoebe, but I realised that losing you is just as bad. It hurts like hell. Even more so because I know it's my fault it didn't work out between us."

Pierce looked at him thoughtfully. "Did you really ask Francis to teach you how to submit because you thought it was what you had to do to be with me?"

Noah shrugged. "Well, originally I just went to see him because...uh, I thought maybe he'd tell me how you were and if I'd really blown all my chances with you. Then we started talking and I realised I had some serious issues. Somehow one thing led to another and suddenly I found myself pouring my heart out to a guy in leather and studs." He smiled.

Pierce chuckled. "Yeah, well, France tends to have that effect on people. I still can't believe you turned to a Dom, of all people, to sort you out."

"Your brother is good at what he does," Noah said earnestly, then grinned. "At least as far as the psychological part is concerned. I suppose if I ever turned to a Dom for, um, professional reasons, it would still be him, though." He shook his head. "But somehow I can't really see that happening. Besides, I'm hoping to get involved with someone who keeps me on a very short leash." He looked at Pierce with a hopeful smile on his face.

Pierce returned the smile doubtfully. "Do you really want that?"

"Pierce, baby—er, darling, I love you and you're the best thing that has ever happened to me. Yes, I want to be with you and I'm willing to do pretty much anything you want to get you back. Just say the word."

The tentative, pleading expression in his eyes went straight to Pierce's heart. He sighed. "Okay. If you want this to work, if you really want us to be together, then I think we can make it work. Two things, though. First, it won't always be easy and I expect you to fight a bit harder next time we hit a sticky patch. Second, if you ever cheat on me again, I'll have your balls, is that clear? Now stop looking at me like I'm going to kick your arse. I'm not. I've got far better things to do with it."

He lowered his head for a long, intense kiss. When he pulled back, Noah's eyes were dark with arousal. "Do you ever miss going to the club?" He watched Pierce with a curious expression.

"Not much. The main reasons I went there were sex and Francis. Casual sex with strangers is not high up on my to-do list these days and Francis has barely got time for me anyway since he became my boyfriend's best chum. No, really, all I miss occasionally is a well-built guy dressed in leather and perhaps some of the...equipment they keep there." Oh yeah, he'd really had fun with some of the things they had at the club.

"Guys in leather, huh? I'll keep that in mind then. What...equipment do you like?" Noah's voice had dropped, a sure sign of his arousal. Pierce blinked in surprise.

"Well, it depends on what I want to use it for. Or with whom."

"What would you use with me?" Noah asked straightforwardly.

"With you?" Pierce asked, baffled. "You're like Pandora's Box, aren't you? You're not seriously considering toys now, are you?"

Noah shrugged, smiling playfully. "Why not? What would you do to me if you could do anything you wanted?"

"What I would do to you, my beautiful darling," Pierce started carefully, trying to picture the scene in his head without panting. "I would put you on a big bed and tie you up. I'd love to put a collar on you, just because it looks stunning on you. I'd put your pretty cock in a leather harness for the same reason and because it would keep you from coming. Then I'd fuck you, first with a dildo to stretch you nice and wide for me, then with my dick, slowly, until you come so hard you don't remember your own name."

Noah's breath hitched. "Anything else?"

Pierce looked at him thoughtfully. "I wouldn't hurt you, Noah. Not ever. I'm not even sure if it would be safe to use restraints with you after what...you've been through." He shook his head regretfully. "I'm not into hurting my lovers. I like playing, though, and I like it kinky. But it's your call, baby. If you're happy for me to use any of that stuff on you or tie you to the bed, you'll have to tell me."

Noah considered his answer for a moment. "I think I probably will—sooner or later, if we ever need to spice things up. So far, it seems you liked what we just did."

"Oh, I certainly did. Any chance I'll get to do it more often?"

"Do what exactly? Fuck me?" Noah flexed his legs, pressing their groins together.

"Ungh, yeah."

"I suppose." He felt Noah smile. "If I get that treatment again."

"Does that mean you liked it?"

"Yeah. It was…good."

"Just good?" Pierce nudged him in the ribs and Noah flinched, chuckling.

"Okay, okay. Yeah, I liked it. I'm not going to stop topping altogether, though," he warned, still grinning.

"I'd be deeply disappointed if you did. It's way too good when you pound my arse."

"Ooh, how I love it when you talk dirty," Noah cackled.

"Do you really?"

"Not sure. I don't think you ever did, did you?"

"You'd blush like a virgin if I did."

"Don't challenge me."

"Why not?"

"'Cause you might not be able to handle the payback."

"I can handle a lot."

"I know," Noah grinned lasciviously as he shifted so Pierce lost balance and smoothly flipped him over, rolling on top of him. He lowered his head for a passionate kiss, eagerly exploring Pierce's mouth.

"Fuck, Noah, didn't I just fuck you?"

"You did. Doesn't mean I don't want more, though."

"You're kidding," Pierce gasped.

"No I'm not." Noah pushed against him. No, he wasn't kidding.

"Shit. You're going to wear me out, aren't you?" Pierce had always been impressed by Noah's high sex drive and stamina, but had attributed it to Noah's age. Youth and lack of opportunity. Noah seemed to be determined to make up for what he had missed in the last few years.

"I certainly hope so."

"What exactly do you think you're doing?"

"Relax, baby. It's my turn," Noah whispered, swallowing Pierce's faint protest in a passionate kiss.

"Think you can really pull it off again?"

"You know I can. By the way, I love you."

"I love you too, but you will be the death of me—oh," Pierce gasped as Noah dipped a naughty, slick finger into him and started twisting it inside him. "Oh yeah, this is good."

It became even better when Noah substituted cock for fingers and fucked him into a second, mind-blowing orgasm.


"Noah?"

"Yeah?" Noah sighed sleepily.

"There's something I forgot to bring up earlier," Pierce whispered into the semi-darkness.

"I think you brought up everything there is very nicely, my darling." Noah grinned, snuggling closer to Pierce.

"I'm serious, Noah."

"What is it?" There was an apprehensive undertone in Noah's sleepy voice.

"You do realise that you'll have to meet my parents eventually, don't you?"

"Meet your parents?" Noah repeated doubtfully.

"Yes."

"Why?"

"Because they're my family and they mean a lot to me. I want you to get to know them."

"You know I'm not exactly good with parents," Noah said reluctantly.

"So what? They're nice people. Besides, Mum is probably going to kill me if I don't bring you around for inspection pretty soon."

"Hm, well now, we wouldn't want that to happen, would we?" Noah grumbled. "How much have you told them?" he asked after a moment.

"About what?"

"About what happened between us."

"Everything." Pierce grinned. "I did edit our sex life, though. Francis is the only one who knows every gory detail about that."

"Ha ha. Great," Noah groaned humourlessly. "What do you think they'll make of us being back together?"

"They'll love you," Pierce assured him.

"After all I put you through?"

Pierce sighed. "If I can forgive you, Noah, they certainly can. Anyway, they're really easy going, you know. After all, they raised Francis," he added with a smirk.

"I suppose I haven't really got much choice, have I?"

"No, not really," Pierce stated.

"Well, then I guess I'm going to meet them after all."

"Fine. Got plans next Sunday?"

"I suppose I do now," Noah said unhappily.

"Good. I'll let Mum know we're joining them for dinner."

Noah tensed. "At their place?"

"Of course. Why, anything wrong with that?"

"Just that… Well, can't I just join you for your Friday night dinners at the restaurant? Or aren't you doing those anymore?"

Understanding, Pierce sighed. Noah wasn't ready for the big meet-the-family thing. "You want neutral territory. This is you meeting me halfway again, isn't it?"

"Yes." Noah looked at him pleadingly.

"Friday night it is then," Pierce confirmed.

# Chapter Eighteen

"Thank you, baby," Pierce said quietly.

"What for?" Noah asked.

"Being here."

"I said I'd come, didn't I?"

Pierce nodded. "I know this isn't easy for you, though."

Noah shrugged, trying to look nonchalant. "I've been through worse."

Smiling, Pierce reached across the table to take Noah's hand. "Relax. They'll love you. Here, have some more wine."

"Are you trying to get me pissed?"

"No." Pierce grinned. "Why, would you like me to?"

"It might make this easier." Noah sighed but shook his head, absently transforming his napkin into a small heap of dark green tissue shreds.

Pierce watched him proudly. Noah had come a long way in the past two months. Pierce knew that Noah would have accepted any date for meeting his parents but had decided to give him some more time to settle into their relationship after all. Although Noah still tended to take the lead, he had become a lot more relaxed and was less determined to stay in control, both in and out of the bedroom.

Out of it, he had accepted that Pierce did things in his own way and was happy to let him make decisions for both of them. In it, he had begun to trust Pierce to the point where he was no longer uncomfortable with allowing Pierce to fuck him, and had even invited him to do it occasionally. Overall, he had become much more affectionate and physical. He appreciated Pierce's touches and kisses, returning them willingly. He also kept his promise of telling Pierce that he loved him at least once a day.

"Hello, darlings!"

The cheerful voice of his mother brought Pierce back to the present. Noah had jerked his hand back as soon as she'd approached their table and glanced up at her with wide, suspicious eyes.

"Hello, Mum." Standing up, Pierce gave his mother a hug and kissed her on both cheeks. "Where's Dad?"

"Parking the car. The car park's frightfully crowded, so he let me out at the front door and took the car to someplace down the road." Turning to Noah, she greeted him with a warm smile. "So you're Noah. I'm so pleased to finally meet you, you wouldn't believe it! Darling Pierce has kept you such a very well-guarded secret, you know."

Having stood up too, Noah had unsuccessfully tried to melt into the background. Finding himself suddenly the centre of attention, he cleared his throat and stuck out his hand. "Mrs Hollister. Nice to meet you," he said formally, visibly uncomfortable. He looked as if he was about to bolt when she grabbed his hand with a girlish laugh and flung herself at his neck in a flurry of waving scarves and perfume, giving him a tight hug.

"There's absolutely no need for Mrs Hollister, dear," she beamed when she released him. "You're family, so please call me Janet."

"Janet," Noah repeated hollowly. He squirmed as she looked him over with open admiration, still holding his hand in hers.

"My, my, Noah," she crooned. "Pierce said you were handsome, but that wasn't doing you justice."

"Mum!" Pierce protested.

"Sorry, darling." She grinned. "I'm just so excited at getting to meet your man at last. Oh, here's your father." Spinning around, she beamed at her husband, Noah's hand still firmly cradled in hers. "Darling, this is Noah. Isn't he gorgeous?"

Her husband looked at her with his usual indulgent smile. "He is, Janet. Now please let the poor sod off, you're making him uncomfortable."

"Oh, I am, aren't I? Silly old me. Just ignore me, dear. I've been over-excited all day." She laughed and finally let go of Noah's hand, leaving him perplexed.

Instantly, Pierce's father gathered him up in a second hug. "I'm Gordon," he said kindly. "Never mind her, son. I can assure you, she is always like that, but entirely harmless. You will get used to it."

Noah's eyes wandered from one to the other nervously. "I, er…yes," he said, baffled.

"So, have you ordered yet?" Janet asked, rearranging her scarves as she finally sat down.

"No, of course not, Mum. We're waiting for you, as always." Pierce grinned as Noah shot him an accusing look behind his mother's back and blew a kiss back in Noah's direction.

"Oh, I see." She briefly glanced at the menu and sighed. "I really can't be bothered to look at that. I'll just have whatever you're having, love." She shifted her attention to Noah, who had once again ineffectively tried to become invisible. "Noah, dear, Pierce said you have a daughter. Why didn't you bring her? I would have loved to meet her."

"Well, um, she...er..." Noah stammered, looking a little overwhelmed.

Pierce cut in smoothly, "It's past her bedtime already, Mum."

"Oh, of course. We'll have to meet earlier next month, so you can bring her. I'm sure she's a perfect little angel. Very pretty, if she's inherited your looks."

"Mum," Pierce groaned.

"What?" she huffed. "Aren't I allowed to be happy? After all, I had already given up on the idea of ever having grandchildren."

"Mum!"

She looked at Pierce dismissively. "Why don't you talk business with your father, darling, while I have a lovely chat with your Noah? So tell me, Noah, was it a problem for you to keep her? It's still a bit unusual for the father to raise the child, isn't it?"

"Maybe," Noah said quietly, shaking off his initial intimidation. "But I'm glad I had the chance to keep her with me."

"Oh, I'm certainly glad you did." She smiled. "Seriously, you would have thought at least one of my sons would start a family. There's really nothing wrong with having a gay son, but both of them?" She sighed. "Well, now, that can't be changed." Reaching across the table, she gently took Noah's hand. "Pierce told me about...your parents. I'm deeply sorry it didn't work out between you. I know you must think

I'm just a frightfully intrusive old bag, but I really don't understand how parents can treat their own child like that. They should be so proud of you for taking responsibility for your little girl. I certainly would be. I just want you to know that, and I'm sure Gordon fully agrees with me on this, I'd be delighted if one day you could come to consider us your family."

Noah stared at her wordlessly, surprise and confusion plainly written across his face. Just then, the waiter appeared with their food. Janet seemed to understand that Noah had had all he could take for the time being and delightedly tucked in, smoothly joining Pierce and Gordon in their talk of business matters. Throughout the evening, Noah was still on edge, but relaxed more and more. By the time they left the restaurant, he was almost his usual self again.

# Chapter Nineteen

Predictably, the wine they'd had with their dinner had left Noah extremely horny, so it didn't come as a surprise when he suggested they go to Pierce's place. The glitter in his eyes told Pierce exactly what he had in mind.

Noah's hands were on Pierce's body as soon as the door clicked shut behind them. "I want you," Noah growled, hungrily kissing a line from Pierce's mouth to his neck. "Let's go to bed." He barely backed off enough for Pierce to manage stumbling up the stairs. In the bedroom, he pushed Pierce onto the bed and climbed on top, finding his mouth and kissing him passionately. Pierce chuckled. "Relieved that it's over?" he whispered into the kiss.

"You bet," Noah grumbled. "Can I get my reward now?"

"Your reward? I wasn't aware you were promised one," Pierce teased.

"Surely you know I deserve one." Noah's tongue found the sensitive spot below Pierce's ear, sending delicious shivers down his spine.

"Ungh, well, let's see..." Pierce moaned. "Anything particular you have in mind?"

"Uh-huh." Noah nodded, nibbling Pierce's collarbone. "I wanna fuck you senseless."

"Oh, that. Well, we haven't done that in a while, have we?"

Noah pulled back and stared at Pierce, feigning offence. "Is that a complaint?"

"No, just a statement." Pierce smiled. "I can remember the last time you fucked me very well, so you obviously haven't succeeded with the senseless bit for a while."

Noah looked down at him. "Fuck, if you can still come up with such thoughts I'm doing something seriously wrong here."

"I don't mind you setting it right, you know," Pierce teased.

"Fine. I will."

Noah didn't need another invitation. He undressed Pierce quickly but sensuously, kissing every inch of skin he bared. His mouth travelled all over Pierce's body, licking and caressing before it zoned in on his aching cock. Running his tongue around the sensitive tip, Noah made him wait for a few sweet moments before he swiftly took him in all the way to the root. Pierce moaned at the relief the touch of velvety moisture promised even if he still had to wait. They were taking it at Noah's pace, and Noah never failed to prepare him with utmost attention until he was convinced that Pierce was ready for him.

By that time, Pierce was usually close to begging for it. One hand on his hips kept him from simply thrusting up into Noah's warm mouth. The gentle pressure against his hole had him moaning again, louder. Noah's skilful fingers invaded him, urgent but careful as always, and Pierce could feel the need in the shallow, shaky breaths Noah took.

At last, Noah released Pierce's cock and leaned across the bed to get the lube. He slicked himself but hesitated before he pushed in. The sweet pressure of the cock on the verge of entering him only added to Pierce's excitement. Looking up, Pierce met Noah's eyes. Dark with arousal, they were also brimming with emotion. There was the faint line of a frown on Noah's forehead, so soft it could easily be missed, but Pierce would have known it was there even if he didn't see it.

"I love you," Noah whispered.

"I love you too." Holding Noah's gaze, Pierce concentrated on the slow progress of the intrusion. There was that slight burn of the stretch as the hard cock filled him, inch by inch, then the short phase of stillness when Noah waited for him to adapt, followed by, at last, the long-desired movement. Noah soon set up a nice rhythm, his thrusts getting faster quickly as their mutual desire built. Soon they were both sweating and groaning, lost to everything but the feel of their bodies working together, thrusting and grinding until they finally spasmed in those few, cherished seconds of pure bliss. They remained glued together for a long time afterwards, kissing and simply enjoying the feel of each other's skin. Eventually, Noah pulled out and settled on Pierce's side, offering him his shoulder as a pillow.

"Go on then," he said after a moment.

"What with?"

"What you want to ask me, of course."

"What makes you think I want to ask you something?"

There was a grin in Noah's voice as he answered. "I just know you, baby. You're dying to get it out."

Pierce smiled into Noah's chest, enjoying the relaxed atmosphere of intimacy between them.

"Well, what do you think?" he asked.

"They're...nice," Noah said thoughtfully.

Pierce was surprised. "You think so?"

"Yes." Noah nodded. "Your mum is, um, intense, but she's nice. Warm. Affectionate." He smiled as he said the last word. "She might be the first woman I like being hugged by."

"Really? The way she crowded you, I was worried you'd make a run for it before the food even arrived."

Noah shook his head. "Actually, it was nice. The way she—well, both of them, I guess——just welcomed me into your family... You're very lucky to have parents like them, do you realise that?"

Pierce considered the question. "I guess I am, aren't I?"

"Yes."

"Well, you heard what Mum said. You can be a part of it. But, mind you, Francis comes with the lot," he warned jokingly.

"I know."

"You two get along really well, don't you?"

"He's a great guy," Noah confirmed. "I like the way he listens to just about anything you say without judging."

"I hope I don't need to worry about him stealing you away," Pierce teased, and stretched to put a possessive kiss on Noah's mouth.

When Pierce released him, Noah smiled. "No. I'm yours. Exclusively. I just started thinking, you know..." he said slowly.

"What about?"

Noah shifted and pushed up on his elbow, looking down on Pierce with an unreadable but serious expression on his face. "Family and...options."

"Oh. Care to explain that a bit further?" Pierce asked when Noah didn't continue.

"Well, you see...I already have a child."

"I know. I hope you know by now that Phoebe's not going to be a problem for me. I adore her," Pierce answered, equally cautiously. Noah's suddenly grave tone had him expecting the worst.

Noah cupped his cheek with his free hand and brushed his lips in a soft kiss. "I know. And you're a wonderful daddy for her. That's not the point, though."

"What is?"

"Well, your parents seem to like me... You know I come from a strictly Catholic family and, even though I don't see a reunion in, well, ever, I was just wondering... Is there any chance you're going to make an honest man of me at last?"

Pierce felt his heart skip a beat. "What exactly are you asking?"

Noah smiled and took his hand, entwining their fingers. "Will you marry me?"

"You're not doing anything by halves, are you?"

"Nope. Not anymore," Noah said earnestly. "Besides, I'm just trying to make sure the leash you keep me on is very short indeed."

Pierce frowned and shook his head, watching Noah's hopeful smile falter. "I'm not sure about the leash, Noah. It's certainly a good look on you, but to be honest, I think a plain old traditional ring would be far more practical in everyday life."

Noah's face lit up. "Is that a yes?"

"Yes."

Noah hugged him tightly and kissed him passionately. "I love you," he finally said, breathless.

"I love you too."

"We're sappy old bastards, aren't we?"

"Yep." Pierce nodded. "Poor Phoebe. Think she can put up with it?"

"Oh, I'm sure she can." Noah's hand wandered down Pierce's back to cup his arse. "Now, Mr Conway, whose turn is it?"

"Mr Conway? What makes you think I'll take your name?"

"Huh? You're not thinking I'll take yours, are you?"

"Of course you will." Pierce pushed up, trying to roll Noah on his back. "And it's my turn."

Noah held against him, grinning mischievously. "It might be your turn, but my daughter and I share that name and I'd like to keep it that way, thank you very much."

Suddenly changing tactics, Pierce pulled at the arm Noah was using to support himself with and flipped him over. "And I'm running a company. Think of all the letterheads I'd have to have changed."

"So what? You can certainly afford it." Noah frowned then shrugged. "I suppose we could settle for Conway-Hollister, that way we'd both keep our names."

"Hollister-Conway, you mean." Pierce said in between pressing possessive kisses on Noah's mouth.

"Not..." Noah started, but Pierce silenced him with another long kiss.

"Shut up and just let me fuck you until you don't remember your name. That should solve the problem."

Noah struggled to get up again. "But..."

Pierce rolled his eyes and kept holding him down. "Conway-Hollister it is. Will you let me fuck you now?"

"Yes, love." Noah smiled, wrapped his arms around Pierce and pulled him down onto the bed, straight into a long, sensuous kiss.

# About the Author

Sage has been passionate about books from a very early age on and dreamt of writing one for years while working on the day job instead. It took a very persistent character in the company of a treasured Muse to finally get the first novel going. The fact that he was gay came as a bit of a surprise, but it explained a lot.

Ever since, Sage has been the willing slave to all the fascinating guys who just keep queuing up and want their stories told. This has resulted in several manuscripts at various stages of completion, so there's always something to work on - preferably at night when the rest of the house is asleep.

Sage's characters often have a dramatic and sometimes traumatic past and need to battle some demons to be with the one they love. It doesn't hurt that they usually get quite a lot of naughty action along the way!

Sage loves to hear from readers, so go ahead please…

Sage Marlowe loves to hear from readers. You can find her contact information, website details and author profile page at http://www.total-e-bound.com.

# Total-E-Bound Publishing

www.total-e-bound.com

Take a look at our exciting range of literagasmic™
erotic romance titles and discover pure quality
at Total-E-Bound.

23802656R00122

Made in the USA
Lexington, KY
26 June 2013